DEAD MAN

& THE

RESTLESS SPIRITS

LOU HARPER

Ginny,

I love you socks!

Love Harper

First published in the United States in 2012 by Harper Books
First Edition

DEDICATION

I owe a debt to my beta readers and critique partners, Jo, Blaine, Kari, Susan, and Jordan. Their frank feedback made this book better. I thank my tireless editor, Linda Ingmanson, for all her help making this story into what it is now.

CONTENTS

UNWILLING SPIRIT

Chapter One

Dying sucked hairy monkey balls. Even when you weren't the one doing it. Denton hated running into the final moments of strangers. Unfortunately, he couldn't always help it. This particular street corner had been safe a week before. The oversized man now clutching his chest must have died sometime since last Tuesday. Heart attack. Denton felt an echo of panic sweep through him and had to grab on to a lamppost to keep from tumbling onto the pavement too. He barely had 135 pounds for his 5' 9" frame, yet he could clearly feel the mass of flesh weighing him down, squeezing the life out of him. At least it was over fast. The man stopped breathing and his presence faded away, both from the street and Denton's mind. He shook himself and took a few deep breaths before going on his way. As he hurried down the street, he made a mental note to avoid that corner for a few months at least—till the trace of fresh death had had a chance to dissipate.

Denton had a near-death experience as a child, and ever since, he'd had a special relationship with the dead. Since nobody had bothered explaining the rules to him, he had to come up with his own theory: when people died, they left an imprint of themselves during their final moments. The more violent the death, the more tenacious the echo. He could also recognize vampires, probably because they were undead. They saw him as something different too, and gave him the name Dead Man. He and the vamps had a truce, and they gave Denton less trouble than the truly dead. He avoided their psychic footprints as much as possible, but a city like Chicago, with its murders and accidents, had lots of death-spots to navigate around.

The warmth of the sun mixing with a nip in the air on this bright September morning soon brought the spring back into Denton's steps. He could see Joy sitting at the patio of Alice's Tea Room from half a block away. Her blonde pixie cut glowed in the morning light. She noticed him too—her face broke into a wide grin, and she waved her arms in the air. Denton picked up his steps, and a few moments later, they exchanged a hug in front of the café.

"Hey, Slackerino!" She squeezed him.

"Hey, Pumpkin. How're you doing?"

"Can't complain." She pushed a paper cup in front of him. "I got you a cappuccino with extra foam, just the way you like it."

"You're the best." Denton grabbed three sugar packets and dumped their contents into the coffee. Then he reached for three more. As usual, Joy made a mocking face at his indulgence. Everything about her made him think of picture-book pixies. She was petite, perky, and her face, with its button nose, dark eyes, and pouty lips, radiated good-natured mischief.

They'd met many years ago at a design firm where Denton worked as a software engineer and Joy as a graphic designer. Like two misfits in that world of cubicles and office politics, they'd become fast friends.

"Guess who I have news about?" Joy asked, bursting with excitement.

"Bigfoot? Walt Disney's brain? No wait, Zachary Quinto's coming to Chicago to shoot a movie."

"You wish. None of the above."

"Okay, I give up."

"Ike Martinez!"

"No way!"

"Way!" Joy beamed at him.

Ike had been their art director—a talentless prick who had regularly taken credit for the works of others. Finally, he'd had the audacity to sign his name to Joy's design, and presented it to the bosses as his own. Joy had gotten so pissed off, she'd quit. Denton handed in his resignation in sympathy. He'd been sick of the place and on his way out anyway. The two of them had started up their own web design company right after. Their boundless loathing of Ike Martinez was one of the many things they had in common.

Denton wanted to know more. "Details, c'mon."

"Okay, so one of my clients asked if I knew him, so I said, sure I do. It turns out, Ike applied for a position at their company."

"What did you tell the client?"

She broke out in an evil grin. "Everything. Then I gave him names of other people he should talk to. Ike won't be getting the job, you can bet on it."

The thought of the asshole getting his due warmed Denton as much as the coffee did. "Well, that's karma for you. Is this why you summoned me here, to gloat together?" They conducted most of their business online, but Joy was also Denton's closest friend—even if he kept major secrets from her.

"I wanted to see you, stupid. And you need to get out more. It's a beautiful day."

It was indeed beautiful—the trees had started turning color, but the memory of summer still hung in the air like a parting smile.

"You're pale as white bread. I bet you spend all your time playing World of Warcraft," she added.

"Nuh-uh. I kicked the habit a year ago. I get out, I swear."

"You don't look it."

Denton could've told her about his recent adventures trying to identify a murderer. However, the story involved vampires, whose existence Joy was blissfully unaware of. So he just smiled. "Unlike your hair, pale's my natural color."

"You don't like my hair?" She tugged on her platinum bangs.

"I do. It fits you. A couple of fairy wings and you'd be complete."

"Hey! Who are you calling a fairy, twinkletoes? Anyway, I refuse to be criticized by someone with facial jewelry," she said, referring to Denton's eyebrow ring and nose stud.

"It was a compliment," Denton said, flashing his tongue stud just to mock her.

"No wonder you can't find a date."

"Hey, lots of guys fancy my studs—find them stimulating. If you know what I mean." He waggled his studded eyebrow—a move he'd practiced in front of the mirror many times.

Joy rolled her eyes. "Uh-huh. How's your love life?"

"None of your business!"

"That bad, eh? Welcome to the club. Are you still looking to move?" Joy could leap from one subject to another with the agility of a gazelle. Denton didn't mind.

"Yeah, but it's hard to find something in my price range not already occupied by an army of cockroaches." Denton's next-door neighbor had a Chihuahua that could yap for hours at all times of the day. Denton had complained to the neighbor, then the landlord, but both had ignored him. He'd been seriously contemplating Chihuahuacide.

"Well, you might be in luck. Remember my friend Miranda?"

"The lactose-intolerant copywriter?" Joy had tons of friends, and Denton could keep them straight only by memorizing their peculiarities, like the dentist who collected vintage license plates or the math teacher who spent every summer reenacting the Civil War.

"Yeah, her. She's leaving town in a hurry and needs someone to rent her condo."

Denton squinted at her with suspicion. "Is she running from the mob?"

"Worse. She's in love."

"How horrible," Denton said in a tone of mock horror.

"Tell me about it. She'd known this Greg guy for like a month but fell so head-over-heels, she's going to follow him to Papua New Guinea."

"Isn't that on the other side of the world?"

"Thereabouts. He's an ornithologist, on a mission to study the rare red-beaked something or other. Or was it blue-tailed? I forget." She shook her head. "Anyway, she's desperate, and I told her I know someone who'd be perfect. The rent would be only a little higher than what you're paying now, but for a million times nicer place. I lied through my teeth about how neat and tidy you are."

"I'm not untidy."

"Bullshit. I've been to your apartment. I made her believe that code monkeys like you are shy and well-organized by nature, even if they look like scrawny pin cushions. I also let it slip you were gay—she loved that. I dunno why people think gays are neat, but you need to work those stereotypes to your advantage. C'mon, we can go see her right now—it's only a few blocks away. If she likes you, you could move in as early as next week."

Joy's proposal sounded good, too good. Denton narrowed his eyes. "What's the catch?"

"What? No catch." Her voice skipped up a notch, and she looked everywhere but at him.

"Don't lie."

"Oh, okay. The guy next door is creepy."

"Creepy how?"

"I dunno… I only saw him once, but all I could think was, if life was a slasher movie, I wouldn't want to be stuck with him in a cheap roadside motel on a stormy night. Miranda thinks he's stuck-up. She says in three years living next to each other, he's never said more than five words to her."

Denton didn't spook so easy. He had much bigger concerns. "Does he have a dog?"

"No. Only a huge cat."

"Cats I can live with. Let's go."

***

By next Wednesday, Denton was all settled in. Thanks to Miranda leaving her furniture behind, the move had been a snap. It had only taken two trips with the rented van to transfer his clothes and other assorted personal belongings. His old furniture went to the city dump. According to Joy, it had been long overdue. Denton like his new digs—the small one-bedroom apartment turned out to be bright and cozy, and only two blocks from the El station. He didn't drive, so access to public transportation mattered. Still, he slept fitfully on his first night, and then woke up at the crack of way-too-frigging-early, thanks to a couple of horny pigeons. The feathered bastards made an unholy racket on the other side of his bedroom window.

That was how he found himself lounging on the fire escape outside the living room window, just as the sun edged its way up over distant rooftops. Denton cradled his coffee mug with both hands and enjoyed the view. From where he was, on the third floor, it consisted of the street below, other buildings, and a large chunk of blue sky. To his right, his "creepy" neighbor's balcony doubled as a miniature jungle chock full of plants. There were tall ones, short ones, some with vines, and others with flowers. They were all just a bunch of weeds to Denton, and not even the kind you could smoke. Having a green thumb didn't gel with the sinister image Joy and Miranda had painted of his new neighbor. All their gossiping had only made Denton more curious. From checking the mailboxes, he'd learned the guy's name: B. Maurell (apartment 309). What did the "B" stand for? Beelzebub? Denton was dying to meet him—only hoping he wasn't a vampire. They were a headache.

His wish was fulfilled sooner than expected, as the balcony door slid open and B. Maurell stepped out, dressed in a cranberry-red bathrobe. Definitely not a vamp but a rather fine specimen of human male of the tall, dark, and handsome type.

"Good morning, neighborino!" Denton shouted in his best Ned Flanders imitation.

The guy looked at Denton, face inscrutable, staring for two whole seconds before giving a curt nod and turning away. Denton could see why Miranda had called him "stuck-up." While B. Maurell fussed with his plants, Denton took revenge by brazenly ogling him. The bathrobe wrapped around a solid body. His movements were surprisingly graceful. His legs stood bare, and Denton enjoyed the view of muscular calves flexing under olive skin and a sprinkling of dark hair. Oh, and nice feet, with high arches. Denton had a thing about feet. He had a thing or two about many things.

After about ten minutes, B. Maurell retreated into his apartment without as much as a parting glance at Denton. Too bad he'd turned out to be an arrogant prick, because otherwise he seemed the kinda guy Denton could get the hots for. Being pale and skinny—a scrawny runt, as Joy would put it—he had a fatal attraction for men who were his exact opposite.

"Meow!"

Denton had been so absorbed ogling his neighbor, he hadn't noticed the cat. The huge black beast had squeezed himself between two planters and regarded Denton with lazy curiosity.

"What's up, puss, how's it going?"

The cat yawned.

"Bored? I'm sorry. Your owner isn't exactly a barrel of laughs. Too bad, because he's kinda hot." Denton wasn't above talking to cats. And who knows, he might even get overheard.

The cat glared at him with curious green eyes; even his ears twitched forward like tiny radar dishes. Only cats and small children could stare with such shameless focus. Denton did his best to return the glare, but he blinked first. As if gloating at his victory, the cat rubbed his face on one of the bars of the balcony, then turned tail and tiptoed into the apartment.

***

Denton spent the most of the day putting a website together for Joy, making revisions as her comments came in. Working freelance had its downside. You were either crazy busy or you twiddled your thumbs wondering where your next paycheck would come from. Denton's fatalistic attitude toward things in general made him well-suited for this lifestyle.

He put the last bit of code in place, double and triple checked it, then spent half the afternoon slicing and dicing pixelated monsters on the computer. He hadn't lied to Joy—he hadn't played World of Warcraft in over a year, but he hadn't gone completely cold turkey with the computer games. He knew he was fine as long as he stayed off-line. When you went online, met other players, joined a guild, started going on raids, that was when the game took over your life. Occasional off-line games of hack-and-slash quelled his craving for the green fields and scorched deserts of Azeroth.

After defeating one last pack of ghouls, Denton shut off the computer to get ready to go out. He was due to attend a party, to meet real people, and a real monster or two. At times it took special skills to tell one from the other.

The night ended up being more work than fun. To make things worse, he had to hobnob with far too many vampires. None of them tried to bite him—they never did—but they gave him a splitting headache. Probably because he saw them in a double vision, even stone sober. He couldn't imagine what it would be like to see them when he was drunk.

Denton didn't get home till late and with the seams of his skull wanting to split. He took a handful of aspirins and went to bed. When he cracked open his eyelids the next day, the sun preened high in the sky, letting him know it was too late to catch his neighbor watering the plants. Oh well, tomorrow would be another day. He pulled the pillow over his head and turned to his other side. Or would've, but his feet didn't budge. Something held them in place. He pushed himself up to his elbows only to see a large, black, furry shape sitting on his bed. After a moment of panic and confusion, his still-groggy brain sorted out that it wasn't a small leopard, only his neighbor's fat feline.

"Yo, cat," he mumbled.

The animal in question hopped off the bed and strolled out of the room. Denton tottered after it a little while later, and bee-lined for the coffeemaker. Fortunately, he'd remembered to fill it up and set the timer the night before, so he didn't have to fumble with it now. He let out a satisfied sigh as the sweet caffeine hit his system.

"Meowrr!" The cat planted its substantial behind in front of the fridge, with an expectant gleam in its eyes.

"Do you have a name, buddy?"

The cat made a deep, throaty noise which sounded kinda like *murr*. It occurred to Denton, if cats could write, their alphabet would have hundreds of letters to express every intonation of their voices. "I'll just call you Murry, okay?" Denton took the slow blink as a yes. "Are you hungry?"

"Meow!"

"Okay, let me see if I have something here for you." Denton rifled through the contents of the cabinets. Miranda had been in such a hurry to leave she hadn't bothered to empty them. Good thing too, because if it was up to Denton, they wouldn't have held much more than peanut butter and jelly. He found a squat can behind the rice.

He held it up triumphantly. "You like tuna, Murry?"

"Meow."

Denton opened the can and emptied its contents into a bowl, which he placed on the floor, next to the fridge. Murry fell on it as if he'd been starving—highly unlikely, judging by his girth. Denton filled another bowl with water and put it on the floor too.

While the cat ate, Denton ambled into the living room. One of the windows was open a few inches. He thought he'd closed them all before going out, but he could've been mistaken. He pushed the window up farther and stuck his head out. The distance between his fire escape and his neighbor's balcony had to be a good ten feet at least. It was hard to imagine Murry, as stout he was, soaring over the space, but obviously he had. He must have been after the pigeons that liked to hang out there. He'd been lucky not to miss the ledge—they were three stories up, and even for a cat landing on his feet, it would've been quite a fall. He could've been hurt.

A cold, wet sensation on his leg made Denton yank his head back inside, only to see Murry sniffing him. Denton slammed the window shut before his guest could get the idea to leave the way he came. "You shouldn't be making such big jumps. It's dangerous."

Unaffected by the lecture, Murry hopped onto an armchair and curled into a ball.

Denton pulled on his jeans and walked next door, but his knocks went unanswered. B. Maurell must have been out. Made sense—he sure would've noticed his giant fur ball missing otherwise.

After a shower and a breakfast of sugar-frosted cereal, Denton plopped down in front of the computer in the corner of the living room and checked his email. He found a message from Joy, with instructions for their latest project. That was the other thing about being a freelancer—no weekends. On the other hand, he made his own hours. He downloaded the files from the server and set to work. Setting up the site structure first, he began work on the CSS templates. He prided himself in coding clean and lean. Murry stayed in his chair, curled up in the shape of a furry donut, but his eyes remained open to a slit, as if he was keeping Denton under observation.

Murry didn't as much as twitch a muscle for the next hour and a half, but when he did, he went from sleep to fully alert in half a second. Looking up to see what had stirred the cat, Denton became aware of the faint rattling of keys and a door closing. His neighbor must have returned. Time to meet the surly and mysterious Mr. B. Maurell.

He stood and scooped up the cat. "C'mon, Murry, time to go home. Ugh, you're heavy."

Murry's meow sounded indignant, but he didn't object to being held. Denton made sure he supported Murry's butt with his arm—cats hated dangling, and Murry had plenty to support.

Chapter Two

The man opening the door radiated a presence more intense than a triple-chocolate fudge cake. Seeing him up close, Denton decided B. Maurell couldn't be called traditionally handsome—all his features were too strongly drawn for it—yet it was hard not to be engrossed by his face. Sharp cheekbones and a prominent nose contrasted with sensuously full lips. The heavy brows and shoulder-length black hair lent him a somber air, but his eyes made the biggest impression on Denton. They were as dark as the deepest trenches of the ocean where the sun doesn't penetrate and strange creatures dwell. They also seemed to accuse Denton of unspeakable crimes. Catnapping, to begin with.

Eager to prove his innocence, Denton held Murry in front of him. "I have your cat. He must have jumped from your balcony to my fire escape. I found him sitting on my feet when I woke up."

Murry, a furry peace offering, hung between them for a beat before his owner reached out and took him. Those eyes focused on the cat for a moment, then back on Denton. "You fed him."

For absolutely no reason, a shiver ran through Denton, but he heroically ignored it. "It seemed a polite thing to do, and it's well before midnight. I didn't let him get wet."

B. Maurell either hadn't seen *Gremlins* or had no sense of humor. "He's on a diet." The warm baritone of his voice undermined the gruffness of the words.

"What kind? If it's Atkins, all's fine—I only gave him tuna, no carbs." Denton meant it as a joke and grinned like an idiot to bring the point home, but all he received in return was stony silence. *Tough crowd.* It was the point to turn around and leave, but he couldn't—the other man's eyes pulled him in with the force of magnets. He had to draw out the encounter any way he could. "I'm Denton. Denton Mills. Just moved in a few days ago. Renting the place from Miranda—she had to leave town in a hurry. Nothing to do with the mob, I've been assured. She said nice things about you, but not your name."

Another tick of measured silence hovered between them; then the sensuous lips parted. "Bran. Bran Maurell."

Such an unexpectedly normal name. Bran Maurell was a man of puzzling contradictions, and Denton loved puzzles. He wanted to know more. Murry, on the other hand, had clearly become bored with the whole affair. He twisted, and a second later, he was on the floor, trotting into the apartment, tail held high.

"Bye, Murry!" Denton shouted after him.

For the first time since the door had opened, the hint of an actual emotion, possibly surprise, registered on Bran's face. "What did you call him?"

"Murry. Not like Bill Murray. Without the 'A.' I asked him his name, and he made kind of a *murr* sound, so I figured I'd call him Murry. *Cat* is too impersonal, don't you think?"

The inner corners of Bran's eyebrows twitched up. "His name is Murmur, but if he didn't object to being called Murry, it's fine."

"Object?"

"He would've let you know." The words were as solemn as the man uttering them.

"Umm. Okay."

Bran stepped forward. "Thank you, Denton, for bringing Murmur home." He held out a hand, and Denton automatically met it with his own.

Bran Maurell had a confident grip. In Denton's experience, hands were usually just hands, but not in this case. The fleshy pads of Bran's palms awakened in Denton a sudden desire to feel them on other parts of his body. Sadly, Bran gave one last squeeze and let go. As he pulled back, a tendril of strange scent brushed against Denton's face—smoke and something fragrant but not flowery. The door closed with a click.

***

The encounter left Denton running hot and cold, and thoughts of Bran kept invading his mind. And not only because Denton was horny and lonely. He thought he'd glimpsed something else under Bran's reserved surface, and it wouldn't leave him alone. Bran Maurell was an enigma smothered in gravy.

When Joy called to discuss details of their newest project, Denton mentioned the meeting but said nothing about his conflicted feelings. If anything, he focused on Murry.

Joy wasn't fooled. Like a barn owl on a mouse, she swooped in on his secret. "You like the guy, don't you?"

"I…umm…he's interesting."

"Riiight. Listen here, Denny boy, you better find out who you're dealing with before you lose your heart and possibly other organs. He reminds me of an ex of mine. Mickey was the same, nose up in the air. I had all these romantic notions of him being Mr. Darcy, but he turned out to be just another arrogant prick. I was young then. I'm much wiser now. When somebody acts like a prick, that's because he is one."

"Okay, old lady. Maybe Bran has one of those social anxiety disorders."

"Uh-huh. Look, Den, go for the guy if you want—God knows, you need to get laid—but don't get in over your head till you get to know him better. That's all I'm saying."

"Thanks for your concern about my sex life."

"It's what friends are for. Hey, do you even know if he's gay?"

"Oh, I know. What I don't know is if *he* knows."

"That could be a problem."

"He's not easy to read."

"Well, he has an interesting face with lots of character— I'll give you that. And it's a good sign he has a cat. Stay away from cat haters—they're all control freaks."

"Thanks for the advice, *Mom*."

"Shut up, and be smart."

It was easy for her to say. Denton had never been smart about guys, always falling for the ones who wouldn't give him the time of day, who thought he was too weird. Or if they didn't, they were already seriously involved with someone else. The last guy he'd had the hots for was shacked up with a vampire.

The next morning, Bran returned Denton's cheerful greeting with a lackluster, "Morning," before turning away and ignoring him. Denton knew he should ignore the guy right back, but instead he spent the next ten to fifteen minutes ogling Bran, imagining various scenarios of wardrobe malfunction caused by freak gusts of wind. Before retreating into his apartment, Bran flashed his eyes at Denton, who almost had an attack of guilty conscience. Bran couldn't have known what had played through Denton's mind, right?

They ran into each other a week later in front of the Balmoral—their building had had the name since its days as a hotel back in the twenties and thirties. At the time of this encounter, Denton was too distracted to pay proper attention to Bran. In addition to death traces, he also encountered what he called ghosts. He saw them as no more than murky shapes hanging in the air, but considering his special connection to the dead, it stood to reason they too were remnants of the no-longer living. Aside from being there, visible to him alone, they didn't do much. One of them happened to be a regular presence by the main entrance of the Balmoral. Any other time, Denton would've simply walked past it. However, on this occasion the shadow was doing something strange. It shook and vibrated as if agitated. Denton had only seen this sort of spectacle once before.

He became so absorbed by the phenomenon, it took him a while to realize Bran was scrutinizing *him* with equal attention. Denton did a quick recovery. "Hi, there. Nice day, isn't it?" He circled around the perturbed apparition and headed for the door.

"Yes," was all Bran said, but he kept his eyes on Denton for the whole three floors in the elevator. It wasn't a friendly look, more like one you give to a rare but ugly bug under glass.

Denton glared back at the sexy prick. Before he could think of something smart to say, the elevator jerked to a halt, the doors opened, and Bran was gone without a parting word. All he left behind was that smoky fragrance.

Denton wanted to kick himself and spent a whole afternoon thinking up opening lines in case the opportunity presented itself again. It happened sooner than he expected. Returning home from running errands the very next evening, he found Bran leaning against the wall between their doors. He wore a black button-down shirt and baggy black jeans. Denton realized, aside from the bathrobe, so far every time he'd seen the other man, Bran had been dressed in all black. Was it some affectation, or did he simply know it looked good on him? Because it did— except for the loose fit of the jeans. That was criminal.

"Good evening, neighborino," Denton said with a friendly smile, not leering at all.

Bran's expression turned surprised—no doubts about it this time. He pushed himself off the wall, and for a nanosecond, he seemed to flicker. Denton chalked it up to a trick of the fluorescent lights.

For a change, Bran appeared more flustered than arrogant. "Hey. I, umm, realized I hadn't thank you properly for rescuing *Murry*. Would you like coffee? Or tea?"

Denton could feel his face splitting into a grin. "Coffee will do."

***

Bran's place was bigger than Denton's, and it also had more windows.

"It's a corner apartment, right?" Denton asked as his host placed a tray of coffee, cream, and variety of sweeteners on the coffee table in front of him. Denton sat on the wide leather couch with his back to the balcony. The greenery spilled inside, continuing the jungle theme. He could smell their complex fragrance from the door, but it got stronger where he sat. It wasn't unpleasant.

"Yes." Bran settled in a chair across the table, eyes glued on Denton, who dumped brown sugar and cream into his cup.

Denton realized if they were to have a conversation, he'd have to work for it. "You have a lot of plants."

"Mostly herbs—in the botanical sense of the word."

Denton, who was clueless about plants in general, had no idea there were multiple definitions of the word and was about to ask, but Bran spoke first. "You work from home?"

"Yes, web development. Joy and I have been at it for a few years now. You might have seen her. Looks like a pixie. Joy's the one who hooked me up with this apartment. She and Miranda are friends."

Bran nodded. "Yes. I remember her. Short, blond, and full of energy."

So Bran didn't completely ignore other people, he only appeared to. Denton thought it was a promising sign. "What do you do?"

Bran sipped his coffee as if he needed time to decide the answer. "I'm a writer."

"Really? What do you write about?"

"Herbs."

"Oh. Well, that makes sense."

They were back to a subject Denton knew nothing about. Conversational quicksand stretched ahead, but Bran stood and walked to the bookshelves taking up most of one wall. He brought back a large hardcover and placed it in front of Denton. He even plopped down on the sofa.

The dustcover was thick matte paper the color of old parchments. A beautiful pencil drawing of a leafy plant and red flowers took up most of the front.

One thing was off, though. "Hey, it says here the author is Fey Blue."

"Pseudonym. My publisher suggested it. Readers trust female witches more."

Denton had been so busy admiring the cover graphic, he totally missed the title: *Herbs for the Modern Witch*. Okay, it was…unexpected, but it took more than casual sorcery to faze him. "So you're a witch?"

Denton squinted sideways at Bran, who returned it with his usual aplomb. "I moonlight as one on occasion. Mainly, I consider myself an herbalist."

Bran leaned forward, and their bodies nearly touched as he observed Denton flipping through the pages. From such close proximity, Denton could feel the heat of his body, and the awareness of it made concentrating on anything else difficult. However, he wanted to do the book justice. Every chapter started with an article about a given herb, presenting its scientific details, then giving various amusing anecdotes of its uses over the ages. Recipes and instructions for its use in spell-casting and potions followed. Drawings in the same style as the cover broke up the blocks of text.

"Nice illustrations," Denton noted.

"The one on the cover and a few others are from my grandmother's notebook. I did the others in the same style."

"Wow, you can draw. These are beautiful." Denton meant it too. He had no artistic skills, and he admired those who did.

A specter of a smile softened Bran's expression, and for a moment, Denton was sure Bran was going to lean closer and kiss him. The illusion shattered as Bran pushed himself off the sofa and got busy clearing away the coffee paraphernalia.

Denton figured it was the signal for him to shove off, so he slammed the book closed, harder than necessary, and stood. He made the customary I-must-be-going noises, and Bran made no effort to keep him. If anything, he seemed keen to be rid of Denton. But then, just as Denton stepped out the door, Bran laid a hand on his shoulder. The action startled Denton so much, he simply stared at the hand—a few dark hairs on the first knuckles. Only when Bran let him go did Denton look into the man's face.

"I'll be practicing my *witchcraft* tomorrow morning, crosstown. You could come and observe, if you wish."

"Okay."

"Good, I'll knock on your door at nine thirty."

Once again, Denton found himself staring at the closed door and the brass numbers spelling out 309.

"Holy mixed signals, Batman," he whispered to himself before heading to his own apartment.

Chapter Three

Next morning, Denton dressed with care. He put on a dark T-shirt with a graffiti-style graphic on its front. The cotton hugged him tight, a good fit with his skinny jeans. There was no use hiding his wiry body, so he played it up. Some guys were into it, so he'd been told.

Bran wore all black again, complete with a lightweight long coat, the lining of which flashed deep red as he moved. Impressive dramatic effect, Denton had to admit. As Bran's gaze slipped from Denton's face to his chest and to the clearly visible outline of a nipple ring through the thin fabric, Denton smothered a satisfied smirk.

Bran snatched his gaze away and adjusted the canvas messenger bag on his shoulder. "It's nippy out there. You should put on a coat."

Denton scowled at him but grabbed a jacket. They went downstairs to one of the few, and much coveted, covered parking spots in the basement of the building.

Denton didn't know much about cars, but he knew enough to see Bran's was one of the less glamorous classics. He spotted a familiar logo on the hood. "I wouldn't have figured this for a Volkswagen."

Bran patted the hood. "Karmann Ghia—was quite popular in its day."

The funny little car made Denton think of a cartoon French man with a pencil mustache. "Cute."

Bran unlocked the doors, and they got in. "My mother's. She left it behind when she moved to California. I don't drive it often. What do you have?"

"I don't drive. I have episodes." Yeah, like episodes of running into other people's final moments, which could make driving dangerous, but he wasn't going to disclose that detail. People simply assumed he meant epilepsy. It scared some off. Good riddance. The truth would've spooked them more.

Bran didn't look bothered, but then again, he was a closed book. His voice sounded calm too. "Is there anything I should know?"

"Like what?"

"What do I do if you have an episode?"

"Just don't let me fall down, but it rarely gets that bad."

"All right." Bran fired up the car, and they were off.

They pulled up in front of Sparks, one of the hot new restaurants in town. Denton had heard about the place from Joy. A CLOSED sign hung on the door. They parked by the curb, behind a late-model silver Mercedes. A paunchy and nervous middle-aged man popped out of it the moment Bran turned off the engine.

"You're here at last," the man said in an anxious tone. A fine sheen of sweat covered his bald head.

Bran calmly stepped forward. "Morning, Mr. Sparks. Is everything prepared as I asked?"

"Yes, yes, of course, to a T. You know, I'm not normally superstitious, but I'm at the end of my rope. I've lost two sous-chefs and a dozen other kitchen staff in six months, and now my chef, Marco, is threatening to quit. Hannah recommended you, and she's not a fool, so why not, right? What have I got to lose?"

The torrent of words crashed against Bran, who remained unmoved. "Of course. Come back in an hour. We'll be all done by then." Probably catching the flash of suspicion in Sparks's eyes, he added, "Or you can wait here.

Either way, my assistant and I need privacy for the next hour."

Sparks blushed. "I'll come back. You've been highly recommended."

Bran gave a curt nod and, with Denton in tow, walked into the restaurant. The tables sat in neat rows in the empty dining room.

"So I'm an assistant now?" Denton asked.

"You are. Take this." Bran pulled a spray bottle—the kind he used on his herbs—out of his satchel and, twisting its nozzle, handed it over to Denton. It was full of yellowish liquid. "Spray it lightly on the walls and tables as we go around the room."

"What is it?"

"Four Thieves Vinegar."

Denton made an experimental spritz and sniffled. "Smells like salad dressing."

"It's good for that too."

"You tried?"

"Yes."

"What are we doing here?"

"The restaurant is supposed to be haunted, so we'll do a cleansing. Also called smudging."

Bran pulled a stubby white candle out of his satchel, placed it on a table, and lit it. Next he took out a bundle of dried herbs firmly tied together. "Sage," he explained. He held the bundle over the candle, but when the flames caught, he blew those out, leaving the sage to smolder and emit a wispy, aromatic smoke. Denton realized it was the same scent he'd caught whiffs of before from Bran.

Bran started from one corner of the room, walking counterclockwise and waving the smoking bundle this way and that as he went. The whole time he kept murmuring to himself. At first, Denton couldn't make out the words, but then realized they were not in English. After a while, he recognized their repeating rhythm. The warm timbre of Bran's voice and the cadence of the chant felt calming and comforting to Denton. He walked a few steps behind and squirted the magic vinegar on the walls and tables. He felt a touch silly doing it, but since nobody could see them, he didn't mind.

By the time they'd done the whole room, the pungent odor of vinegar mixed with the more fragrant one of the herb. "Sparks will have a job explaining the smell to the customers."

"The windows don't open, but the AC will take care of it. Eventually," Bran said and headed to the door leading to the kitchen.

As soon as they stepped inside, Denton spotted it—thick and dark like coal smoke, the shape hovered next to the walk-in freezer at the other end of the kitchen.

Bran didn't appear to be in a hurry. "Back in the sixties, this place was an Italian restaurant, a small family place. The owner had friends in the mob. One of them was Vinnie Pagano, a hit man for the Attanasio family. A true cold-blooded killer. According to rumor, he fell out of favor when he got Pasquale Attanasio's daughter, Antonia, pregnant. One night, as he left the restaurant, through the kitchen as always, he was gunned down right outside. He had just enough strength to drag himself back inside before dying." He stopped and looked at Denton as if expecting something.

"It sounds like a campfire ghost story. Are you trying to scare me? Because it's not working."

Bran shook his head and went on being atypically chatty. "It's all true. I always do my research before taking on a job, so I know what to expect. I know somebody at the Chicago Historical Society." His gaze swept through the kitchen and settled on Denton. "Do you see anything? Tell me."

Denton almost told him about the shape looming on the other side, but his paranoia kicked in—it felt like a trap. "I see nothing but an empty kitchen."

"All right. We go the same way as in the dining room." He set off to his right and made his way around, as before.

Denton kept spraying, but from the corner of his eye, he kept a watch on the dark shadow, which behaved more and more strangely as they drew near.

The walk-in freezer stood a few feet from the shadow's current location. Bran pulled its door open and made Denton stand in the open doorway. "Make sure you stay outside while I'm in there, and don't let the door close." He went in and did his chanting and waving.

Denton leaned on the door; then it felt as if the door leaned back, trying to push him. It had to be the ghost. What a bastard. Denton planted his feet firmly on the floor and stood his ground. When Bran was done, they changed places.

Once the freezer got thoroughly smoked and sprayed, Bran let its door slam shut, but instead of moving on, he stopped again. "The week after Vinnie Pagano's death, Antonia Attanasio married a young baker by the name of Joseph Bertucci. Not quite seven months later, she gave birth to a healthy baby boy. By then the restaurant was gone—destroyed by a grease fire. Ever since, dozens of businesses have opened and closed here. Some disaster always struck them. It stood empty for years—the reason why Roger Sparks got it so cheap. He's not a superstitious man, but things have been going awry from the start. Freak accidents, fresh meat going rancid in a few hours, right in the freezer. Hardened kitchen folk getting the heebie-jeebies. That's why he called me." He sounded a bit as if he was repeating a practiced speech.

"For a guy who normally won't say two words to a person, you can spin a yarn like a pro."

By then, the ghost—because what else could it be?—hovered at the door between the kitchen and dining room. If Bran pressed him now, Denton probably would have fessed up about it, but Bran didn't ask. He just resumed his ritual.

As they got close to the door, the dark gray of the ghost billowed and spiraled, impersonating a miniature tornado. No more than a few feet separating them now, Denton had a much better view. The shape started to become ragged around the edges, large chunks of it fading away. Denton stepped up and spritzed the Four Thieves Vinegar right into the middle of the figure. It shuddered, but then it suddenly surged forward. Denton felt a sudden rush of rage, yet he knew the emotion wasn't his own.

He instinctively held out his free hand, palm open, fingers spread out. With a touch of anxiety, he realized the foolishness of it right away—he couldn't stop an intangible shadow with his bare hand. The gesture, along with his intense wish for the thing to be gone, was pure instinct. What happened next came as a shock. A massive surge of heat filled his whole body, but before he had a chance to be scared, it exploded out of his palm in the form of a flash of white light. The whole event took no more than a second or two, but it obliterated the ghostly shape without a trace. Denton stood dumbstruck, his pulse racing with an odd mixture of relief and thrill—like at the end of a roller-coaster ride. He stared at his hand, but it looked as normal as ever.

Bran made a satisfied hum, as if this was all in a good day's work for him. "We're done," he said and extinguished his sage bundle at a nearby sink. He then went out the back door, leaving Denton in a befuddled mess. With nothing better to do, Denton followed him and found him burying the remainder of the sage under a patch of dirt. He used a gardening trowel, which he neatly sealed in a Ziploc bag before dropping it into his satchel. He also took the nearly empty spray bottle Denton was still clutching.

A series of loud clucking sounds made Denton look up at the tree they stood under, where he caught sight of an impressive black form. "That's one big crow!"

Bran followed his gaze. "Raven. Fat, more like it. A wonder it can even fly."

With a loud and offended caw, the bird spread its wings and took to the air. It flew pretty damn well. Gracefully, even. Soon it disappeared over the roofs.

Bran closed his bag and adjusted it on his shoulder. "Let's go. Mr. Sparks must be anxious."

Mr. Sparks was anxious, hopeful, relieved, and anxious some more, all at once. Bran gave his assurance to the worried restaurateur in his customary terse manner. Curiously, Bran's brusqueness had a calming effect on the other man. Soon Denton and Bran were on their way home.

They spent the trip in an odd silence—not sullen, but not comfortable either.

Denton's thoughts kept jumping around but always returning to the story Bran had told. "What happened to the boy?"

"What boy?"

"Antonia's son."

"Died in a boating accident on the lake at age twenty-three. They say he was a real piece of work, and only his mother grieved over him."

"You're either the greatest bullshitter in the world, or you really did your homework."

Bran turned his coal-dark gaze on Denton. "I don't always tell the truth, but I never lie."

***

Denton was ready to be dismissed the moment the elevator doors opened on their floor, but Bran surprised him again. "It's almost lunchtime. Why don't we order delivery, and while we wait, you can tell me the truth about what you saw in the restaurant."

One corner of Bran's mouth curled up as he looked at Denton, and this hint of a smile tugged at Denton's heart. He ached to see the smile grow. Joy was probably right, and Denton would end up regretting this, but at this moment, he didn't care. He wanted more of this man. Gawd, he was a sucker.

"Okay."

"What do you want, pizza, Chinese, Thai?" Bran asked, unlocking his door.

"Meow." Murry waited for them on the other side, sitting under the coatrack.

Bran gave him a stern stare. "No, most definitely not. It makes you gassy."

The cat glared back at him before standing and rubbing his face on Denton's legs. He bent down and scratched the cat behind the ears.

"He likes you," Bran said, hanging up his coat and kicking his shoes off.

Denton followed Bran's example. He wasn't surprised to see Bran's black socks. His own, on the other hand, were a red-and-yellow-striped pair. Colorful socks had been his weakness since he'd been a little boy. Bran stared at them for a couple of seconds, but then he shook his head and headed to the kitchen for the takeout menus.

"Can I get you a beer?" he asked over his shoulder.

"Sure." Denton followed Murry into the living room, and the two of them settled on the sofa.

Denton rubbed Murry's thick jowls, and the cat expressed his gratitude with a rumbling purr.

Bran came back and handed Denton the bottle, then settled on the other side of the sofa. The setup very much started to resemble a date. Oh hell, he might even get laid. Being an eternal optimist, Denton dared to hope.

At his suggestion, they ordered meat-lovers' pizza with extra cheese, and a six-pack of Dr. Pepper.

"I prefer to drink something sweet with greasy food," he explained.

"You have a sweet tooth."

"Not a crime."

"No. Tell me about the spirit at the restaurant."

"You saw it too, didn't you?"

Bran shook his head. "No. I can sense their presence, sometimes catch a glimpse from the corner of my eye, but nothing more. I truly wish to know how you perceive them."

"Well, it's not always the same, but usually a dark, murky shape, like smoke or shadow. I call them ghosts, because"—Denton opened his eyes big and made his voice gravelly—"I see dead people."

Bran looked back at him with absolute seriousness. "I know you do. There's one in front of our building, isn't there? That's what you were staring at the other day."

"Yeah. It doesn't appear hostile."

"I think it must be Mr. Klusky. He was the doorman here for three decades. Died five or six years ago."

"Talk about taking your job too seriously."

Bran shrugged. "Must be stuck. Do you see anything else besides these spirit shadows?"

"Umm, I see how people died. I read an article once, which said if you leave a body at a spot for twenty-four hours, or even less, a cadaver dog can identify the spot even years later. I'm sorta like that. The best I can figure, when people die, they leave an imprint where it happened, and when I run into it, I re-experience it. Fortunately, they rarely last years. Mostly just a few months."

"It must be unpleasant." Bran leaned forward, and genuine sympathy softened his words.

"No kidding." Denton grimaced, but his heart jumped a little.

"Is it what you call *episodes*? You should be able to buffer them."

Denton opened his eyes wide in surprise. "How? I wish I had control over this thing, but I don't."

Two deep grooves appeared between Bran's brows. The beer must have relaxed his facial muscles. "Hm. Have you always had this talent?"

"No. I had a near-drowning experience when I was nine. It started after."

Bran hummed again, drank his beer, and stared into nothing, brows furrowed for a good while. Finally he stood and got himself another beer, forgetting to even ask if Denton wanted one. "Was there anything unusual about your accident?" he asked, sitting back down.

"Unusual? I dunno. It was winter, I went out on the frozen lake, the ice broke, I fell in. Someone pulled me out. EMT revived me after being under for fifteen minutes or so. Supposedly the cold water saved me." An involuntary shiver shook Denton at the memory of the cold.

"And from then on you could see spirits?"

"Yeah. How long have you been doing this smudging stuff?"

"I did my first when I was five, so it would be over two and a half decades. I was homeschooled for years, and Mother had an unconventional curriculum. Witchcraft has been in my family for generations."

"You must be quite a witch, then. Or is it wizard?"

"Witch. But that's my mother. I prefer herbs."

With a light prodding from Denton, Bran gave Denton the dirt on his herb garden. Denton tried to retain the information, but mostly he simply enjoyed hearing the man talk and watching Bran gently touch a leaf here, fondle a stem there. *Lucky bastards.* No wonder they were the perkiest, most lively plants Denton had ever seen.

A second bottle of beer loosened up Bran some more. When the pizza arrived, he was on his third, and a lot of the starch had gone out of his posture.

He sprinkled chopped green stuff on top of his slice. "Parsley and basil," he explained.

Denton tried it too, cautiously at first, but it tasted fine.

They ate in companionable silence. Denton sneaked a few pieces of meat to Murry under the table.

"Don't complain to me if he pukes on your feet," Bran said.

Denton flushed at being caught. "He's not fat, just big boned."

"Right. Murmur."

The cat slinked out from under the table and hopped onto a chair. He sprawled out with a satisfied smirk on his furry mug.

"You must have been hungry," Bran remarked when Denton finished his fourth slice.

"It's my metabolism. No matter how much I eat, I don't gain weight. Jo says I'm skinnier than a drowned rat—which in my opinion doesn't even make sense. I mean, fat rats can drown too, right? She's just jealous."

Bran took a swig of his beer. "Back when you fell into the lake, who pulled you out?"

"Just some guy… You know, that part was odd. My mom tried to find him to thank him but couldn't. Nobody had seen him around before or after. All she could find out was the guy's first name: Bill. But nobody could even give a detailed description of him. I'd completely forgotten about that part." He felt another brush of chill but shrugged it off.

"Hm, interesting. Very interesting."

"What, you know who he is?" Denton highly doubted it was possible, Bran being a witch or not.

"No, but I have a suspicion about his...nature. I believe he made you into a necromancer when he saved you. I don't know why."

"Necromancer? Like those guys who make zombies and skeleton armies?"

Bran gave him a disapproving look. "No. Don't be ridiculous. That crap is for video games. A necromancer is someone who has a special connection with the dead, who can communicate with them."

"Communicate is stretching it. I can feel them and see them."

"You're untrained."

"And how would I go about getting trained? Not something you can find in the Yellow Pages."

"It's not my area of expertise, but I can ask around. Give me a little time."

"Okay."

"By the way, you can also cast out spirits. You blasted ol' Vinnie straight to the other side."

Thinking back, Denton had to admit it'd been pretty cool. He grinned. "It was me, wasn't it? The whole light show. I have no clue how I did it."

"Instinct. Angry spirits of his sort can be nuisance, but not too hard to deal with. My smudging would've taken care of it, but your method was faster."

"There are different kinds of spirits?

"Of course. Most people cross over when they die, but some can't fully let go, and part of them stays behind and becomes this *thing*. Not a person, but a concentrated emotion—pain, anger, greed."

"You kinda tricked me there, into doing that stuff."

"Yes."

"Why?"

"Because I like you."

Denton, completely unprepared for this answer, sputtered for a moment. "You're not making any sense."

Bran shrugged and took another swig of his beer. Denton had had enough of the arrogant, unpredictable, sexy bastard. He carefully wiped his fingers, downed the rest of his soda, then, with a casual but determined move, he closed the distance between them. He straddled Bran's thigh, threaded his fingers into the thick, black locks, and kissed those sinfully full lips. An empty beer bottle landed on the hardwood floor with a clank, and the next moment, Bran pushed both his hands under Denton's shirt.

They made out for long minutes, kisses deepening, bodies becoming desperate for more contact. With impatient fingers, Denton unbuttoned Bran's shirt. The tawny skin underneath stretched over firm flesh. Denton traced the outlines of muscles with his hands. He could hardly believe he'd gotten this far and that Mr. Aloof hadn't brushed him aside yet. He dug his fingers into the coarse dark hair covering Bran's pecs. "You're so fucking hot."

Even Bran's chuckle was sexy. Escalating the stakes, Denton scrabbled to undo Bran's belt and fly. Dipping his hand inside, he found Bran hot and hard for him, Bran's cockhead sticky with eagerness. He swiped his thumb over the head, and Bran's breath caught.

Bran tried to reciprocate, but Denton's jeans were too tight. "Get them off," he said, tugging at them.

Denton stood up long enough to peel off his jeans and briefs. Bran used the opportunity to arrange himself into a more suitable position on the couch. He also pushed his jeans down a few more inches. He wore a black jockstrap, which Denton found surprisingly kinky. From a thick thatch of dark hair, his cock rose solid and proud. Denton took back his spot, knees on either side of Bran's hips. Bran wrapped his long fingers around both their dicks so Denton's Prince Albert rubbed against the underside of Bran's cock.

Denton thought it delightfully debauched to have frantic, half-dressed sex on the living room couch. He was in his T-shirt and socks, and while Bran technically still had all his clothes on, their disordered state only made him look more wanton. Denton felt outright smug seeing Mr. Cool-and-Composed disheveled and breathing heavily. Then he stopped thinking as the pleasure of skin-on-skin drove everything else out of his mind.

They climaxed seconds apart, making a sticky mess mostly on Bran's chest and stomach.

"Whew." Denton fished his briefs from the floor. It served well enough to wipe off most of the cum. "I can't believe I got you in the sack at last," he said, nestling between Bran and the back of the couch. It was a warm and cozy spot, matching Denton's mood.

Bran had his forearm over his eyes. "This won't end well."

What an odd thing to say, Denton thought. Oh well, he'd think about it another day. Right now he was happy.

HUNGRY SPIRIT

Chapter One

Denton sat cross-legged on the floor of Bran's living room. Both eyes closed, he tried hard to find his third eye—an imaginary spot between his eyebrows that was supposed to fill him with light. According to Bran, anyway. Easier said than done. Denton had never had much luck focusing on anything for long, other than writing code—because code was pure, beautiful logic. With everything else, his mind wandered. Right now his nose itched, and it took all his self-control not to scratch. That, of course, shifted his concentration to the tip of his nose. Maybe his third eye had slipped down there—everything else was screwy about him; why not this? He pictured a tiny eye blinking above his nostrils. Freakish but funny.

"Stop fidgeting!" Bran snapped.

Denton opened his eyes—the real ones—and saw Bran sitting across from him, with an irritated groove between his brows, where *his* third eye would've been. Bran was not happy. They'd been training for weeks, ever since Bran had received a beat-up old book in the mail from his mother. The tome was in Spanish, so Bran had to translate it first. It had been slow going, as the language was archaic. They'd both been busy too—Denton with a difficult website for a difficult client, and Bran had his next book's deadline looming over him. The situation made them both testy. Denton got annoyed with himself for failing, and with Bran for making him do the stupid thing in the first place.

"I didn't move a muscle," he protested.

"You were twitching nose to toe."

Denton looked at his feet. His toes flexed in the orange socks. They had a habit of moving on their own. He rarely noticed it himself. "I can't help it. I never could sit still for long. It used to drive my teachers crazy."

Bran remained stern. "I've noticed. Are you even trying? I thought you wanted to get a handle on your talent."

Denton hated the schoolmaster tone; he hated how it made him feel like a child. His irritation rose. "No, I fucking love getting ambushed by dead people. This is a big joke for me, and I enjoy being lectured and treated like a failure!"

Blankness spread over Bran's face, while the flex of his jaw muscles hinted at some suppressed emotion. Probably annoyance. For a moment, Denton thought they might have their first fight, but Bran simply stood and walked out of the room. What the hell was Denton supposed to do?

A familiar feeling of frustration welled up in Denton. It had become his dominant emotion when it came to Bran. When they'd gotten physical about a month ago, he'd thought it would change things, but it didn't, not really. They were still barely more than neighbors with benefits. While Bran unquestionably took his task of helping Denton to gain control over his necromancer skills very seriously, he kept Denton at arm's length. Even when they had sex, it was always initiated by Denton, ended too quick, and, *fuck*, they never even got properly naked. Jerking each other off while mostly dressed had held a certain kinky appeal at first, but it had quickly become dissatisfying. Bran wouldn't even let Denton blow him, and what healthy man turned down a BJ? Especially since he had no problem with doing it to Denton. Yet whenever Denton pushed for more, Bran clammed up and had somewhere else to be.

If it wasn't for a few curiously tender glances and gestures from Bran, and the fact that Denton truly wanted get better with his talent, he would've bagged it and moved on. But here he was, sitting on the floor like a big fat idiot. Scratch that and make it big skinny idiot. Maybe he had deep-seated psychological issues, getting involved with emotionally unavailable men. Joy seemed to think so.

Bran returned and handed Denton a milky-white globe an inch or more in diameter. His fingers caressingly brushed Denton's palm, and his voice was warm and full of apology. *Bastard.* "I'm not a good teacher. Try this. It might help."

"What is it?" Denton asked, grumbling, reluctant to let go of his disgruntlement.

"Moonstone. Hold it in your hand. Play with it if you want. It might help you concentrate."

"I thought the problem was I couldn't keep still."

"You were scattered. It's not the same thing. You know how I chant when I do a smudging?"

"Yeah, I wondered about that."

"It's a Spanish incantation I learned from my mother. It tells the spirits to leave and never come back, but the ritual would work fine without it. Repeating the words helps me clear my mind from distractions. Half the success of any rite is in using the right tools, going through the prescribed motions. The other half is the medium being in the right frame of mind."

"So anyone who has those could do what you do?"

"No. You either have the talent or not. Same with you. Now close your eyes and feel the stone."

Denton obeyed. The stone was smooth under his fingers. Denton imagined it still being warm from Bran's hand, even if it was heated by his own now.

He decided to visualize it. For some reason, the gem made him think of morning fog—white as the light he was supposed to channel. And there it was, at first barely a fleck, but it grew and filled his field of vision.

Plonk! was the sound of the moonstone slipping out of his fingers and hitting the carpet.

"Sorry!" he said, feeling foolish.

But Bran didn't appear annoyed this time. "Don't be. You were still for a full five minutes."

"I was?"

"Pretty good. We can stop for today."

"Do I get a reward?" Denton rolled forward onto his knees and advanced on Bran, ignoring the *Dirty Dancing* flashback.

Bran leaned forward and cradled Denton's face between his hands. As they kissed, Denton was aware of both the hot, wet tangle of their tongues and the tender caress of Bran's fingers—as if he was communicating with them the things he never said with words. Or maybe it was Denton's wishful thinking.

Bran pulled away. "I can't. I have a manuscript to get back to my editor by tonight."

"Twenty minutes won't make a difference." It wasn't as if they were going to lounge in bed afterwards.

Bran was already pushing himself off the floor. "I…we could go out later."

Now that stopped Denton's thoughts in their tracks. "Out?"

"Yes."

"As in, into a public place with people? Lots of people?" They'd never left the building in each other's company before, well except that one time to do the cleansing.

"I didn't mean a Lady Gaga concert, only dinner."

Denton was dumbfounded. "Dinner?"

"A meal people have in the evening. You like food."

"I know what dinner is. I just didn't think you were sociable enough to have one in a real restaurant."

Bran gave a jerky shrug. "Roger Sparks called. He wanted to express his gratitude."

"And you accepted?"

"He wouldn't take no for an answer."

"I see."

"So, see you at seven?"

***

A witch and a necromancer walk into a bar... Denton shook his head. Those jokes always had trios, and Sparks wasn't a bar. The moment they stepped inside, they were treated like VIPs. The hostess guided them to a cozy corner booth, where they had sparkling water and a wine list on the table before their posteriors had a chance to warm the seats.

Their waitress introduced herself as Ashley and smiled like her life depended on it. She seemed very young, even with her auburn hair pulled into a severe bun. Handing them the menus, she recited the specials and left them alone. A few minutes later, she scurried back to take their orders and kept buzzing around like an overachieving bee for the rest of the night.

Roger Sparks himself arrived alongside the appetizers—grilled calamari salad and crab cakes—not sweating this time, but gushing gratitude. Even Bran's monosyllabic responses failed to dampen the restaurateur's mood. Not long after he'd taken his leave, the entrées arrived—roasted monkfish with risotto for Bran, and New York strip steak with brandy cream sauce for Denton.

Ashley placed the plates in front of them with pride. "Chef Valenti himself made these for you. He asked me to tell you how much he appreciates what you've done for the restaurant. He would've come by to say it himself, but he figures you've been bothered enough already and would probably like to eat in peace." She looked at them, doe-eyed and blushing as she said the words.

Bran remained mute and annoyed, so Denton thanked her and asked to convey their gratitude to the chef.

As soon as she fluttered away, Denton turned to Bran. "Okay, so they are overattentive. No reason to be rude."

Bran twitched an eyebrow. "I wasn't rude."

"Are you saying that was the grand total of your social skills?"

"Probably." He didn't appear in any way bothered by the admission.

Denton pressed on. "Do you go out much?"

"No."

"I must be special, then," Denton said in a teasing tone.

Bran blinked a few times, opened his mouth as if to say something, but then he took a drink of his wine instead. Casting his gaze on his plate, he turned his attention to the pile of rice.

After a few minutes, Denton couldn't take the silence anymore. "I bet Sparks will get you a bunch of new clients."

Bran groaned.

"What's wrong with that?"

Bran stabbed his fish with a fork as if he had a blood feud with aquatic creatures. "I only do the witch stuff because my mother left me her clients when she moved to California."

"You don't like doing it?"

Bran shrugged. "I don't like dealing with people. And I'm not good at it—as you pointed out."

"I noticed. You could just say no."

"Mother would kill me. I charge exorbitant fees to discourage them, but they keep coming back and referring others."

"Sucks to be you."

Denton felt short on sympathy. After all, he was in a similar situation himself—occasionally, he relived the dying moments of other people for money. Unpleasant but preferable to doing it for free. Dealing with live people, on the other hand, he didn't mind at all.

As if reading his thoughts, Bran put his fork down and looked Denton in the eye. "When you learn to control your talent, it'll be easier for you. You'll be able to choose how deeply you experience those death traces and even shut them out completely if you want."

"That would be nice."

"If I were a better teacher, you'd be there by now."

"It's not your fault. I'm too spacey to concentrate."

Bran shook his head. "I'm terrible at teaching. I wish Mom was here. She's so much better at this. At least, she was with me."

"Was your mother a full-time witch?"

"Still is. Only she got tired of cold winters and lake-effect snow." The wine seemed to have loosened Bran's tongue. Denton liked it.

"How does one go about making a living as a witch?"

"Lots of fortune-telling, personal services. Various rituals."

"Like what?"

"Blessings, banishings, you name it. She has a businessman client who won't make a major investment without consulting her."

"She must be good."

Bran leaned back in his seat. "Half of what she does is real. The other half is…theater."

"What do you mean?"

"Cleansing a house from negative spirits has tangible effects. Protection spells, love spells, and the like are not fool-proof, but they can make a difference. However, what people want most is to know the future."

"And nobody can see the future, right?"

"I didn't say that. She…we both have the gift of second sight, but it doesn't work on command. The moments of prescience are random and unpredictable, and often useless."

"Useless how?"

"People want to hear good news. They don't want to know they'll be audited by the IRS."

"So you simply don't tell them?"

"You warn them about watching matters of money, and say things like they'll overcome adversity. You have to put a positive spin on it. Mother is a master at it."

"And you?"

"What do you think?"

"I see. You'd probably tell them the bad news straight out."

Bran played with his glass. "Maybe. What would you do if a down-on-his-luck guy came to you, desperate for good news, and you had a vision of his imminent death? Would you tell him?"

"I…I dunno. What would you do?"

"I told him great fortune and happiness headed his way."

Realizing they weren't talking of a hypothetical situation made Denton uneasy. He had a feeling he didn't want to know the ending of the story yet couldn't help asking, "Did he die?"

"Got hit by a bus a few minutes later. It was quick."

Denton put his fork down. "That's absolutely the worst story I've heard recently, and I've heard a few doozies."

"I'm sorry, but that's life—a series of terrible stories."

He should've just left it, but the fate of the unknown man kept picking at Denton. "If you told him the truth, he could've done something about it."

Bran shook his head. "No. You can't change the future any more than you can change the past. At least this way he had a few minutes of bliss before he died."

The fatalism of those words didn't sit well with Denton, but he didn't want to argue. "What's the point of knowing the future, then?"

"Exactly. And that's why I refuse to tell fortunes anymore."

Ashley swooped down on them, right on cue, asking how everything was, if they needed anything. Bran made a visible effort to return her smile and asked about dessert. Immediately, she began to gush about the chocolate lava cake with cherry sauce and homemade ice cream. It sounded luscious. Denton caught Bran gazing at him, the corner of his mouth curled up, which in his case counted as a smirk. Turning his gaze away, Bran asked the waitress to bring them a lava cake.

"Was I so obvious?" Denton asked.

"You had a look on your face."

"I have a look?"

"When you want something, yes." Bran lifted his glass and gave Denton a hard-to-read gaze over its rim.

"Then you know I want you all the time?"

Bran swallowed hard and cast his eyes down. It was out of character for him to be flustered. "I shouldn't drink. It goes to my head too fast," he said, placing his glass on top of the white tablecloth.

"'That's good. This is the first real conversation we've had. I finally get to know more about you. It's nice."

"What if you don't like what you learn?"

"Doubtful."

Bran gave him a wistful smile. "You sure?"

"Oh, don't be such a drama queen. When we first met, I thought you were an arrogant prick. Your previous neighbor warned me you were the baddie from a slasher movie. But I think you're a nice guy. And when you relax, like right now, you're almost fun."

Bran tilted his head sideways. "Almost?"

"Give it more wine."

Bran touched his fingers to his glass but didn't lift it. Instead, he stared into the chardonnay as if it was a crystal ball.

Ashley arrived and set a plate in the middle of the table. She placed a dessert spoon in front of each of them and wished them "good appetite" before scuttling away. Bran stared at the shiny silverware in front of him.

Denton grinned. "I guess she made us out for a couple."

Bran didn't reply or make eye contact, but he picked up the spoon and used it to slice a neat little chunk of the cake. Dark chocolate oozed out of the fissure, demanding Denton's undivided attention. The cool sweetness of the ice cream balanced the hot chocolate—like yin and yang. The cherry sauce added a playful note. Denton was scraping the plate clean before he knew it. He caught Bran watching him with eyes darker than the darkest chocolate.

It made Denton a bit self-conscious. "Do I have food on my face?"

Bran shook his head. "I enjoy watching you eat."

Denton took care to eat the rest of his dessert as suggestively as one can without being arrested for public indecency.

Chapter Two

A couple of days later, during their next training session, Denton found his third eye without problem, and, according to Bran, he remained focused for close to half an hour. Bran sounded pleased but didn't waste time on accolades. "Next we'll have to work on you channeling the light without being in a meditative state."

"Hm. Sounds tricky."

"Nah. It's similar to taking the training wheels off your bicycle." Bran sprang up from the floor before Denton could trap him. He'd been evasive since the dinner at Sparks, turning down Denton's sexual overtures and claiming to be busy with his book. In Denton's opinion, no healthy male was too busy for a nookie. Something was up.

Apparently, Murry thought so too. "Meoooowrrr." He vocalized his opinion from his roost on the back of the sofa. He stared straight at Bran while doing so. Bran stared back, furrowing his brows in the manner of a man holding back words of disagreement. Murry held his gaze with feline obstinacy. A sharp ringing broke the stalemate. Bran marched out into the foyer to the intercom, and Denton drifted after him.

"Hello?" Bran barked into the device.

A tinny female voice came from the speaker. "Mr. Maurell?"

"Yes. Who's this?"

"Hi, I'm Ash…Ashley. I was your waitress the other night. Can I please come up? I need your help."

Well, that was an unexpected turn of events. Denton watched Bran hesitate, probably fighting his antisocial instincts. Civility won out. "Third floor." He buzzed her in.

A minute later, there was a knock on the front door, and Ashley walked in. She looked younger out of uniform, in jeans and a plain T-shirt, her hair framing her face in lazy waves. The sunlight tangling in her locks brought out their reddish hues. She clutched a small brown purse in front of her as a shield. Bran's glare couldn't have helped her anxiety. The sight of her nervously chewing her lower lip woke a pang of sympathy in Denton. Her lipstick was already in ruins.

Since Bran could be counted on to make her feel more ruffled, Denton resolved to play the role of the host. He ushered her into the living room and over to a comfy chair.

"Can I get you something to drink? Coffee, tea, water? A shot of gin?" he asked.

"Water would be nice," she replied with a grateful smile.

A minute or two later, they were all settled around the coffee table, Ashley on one side, Denton and Bran on the sofa across from her. Murry kept his old post on the back of the sofa.

Ashley perched on the edge of her chair, sipping from her glass, her eyes darting from Bran to Denton. "It smells good in here," she said.

Denton nodded toward the windows. "Herbs." To him, the scent barely registered anymore. "What can we…Bran do for you?" he asked to get the ball rolling.

"I need your help getting rid of a ghost." The words rushed out of her like water from a broken dam. "Uncle Roger bragged to everyone how you stopped the haunting at the restaurant. And you really did!" Her gaze flicked to Bran, then quickly back to Denton. "And you seemed such a nice couple, so I thought…"

Denton glanced at Bran, who seemed engrossed in the study of his cuticles. So he turned his attention back to Ashley. "Roger Sparks is your uncle?"

She nodded with unwarranted enthusiasm. "My mom's brother. You see, I'll be going to school for hospitality and restaurant management next fall. I'm working in Uncle Roger's restaurant till then. My father thinks kids should learn real work before going off to college. I've been doing everything from food prep to washing dishes. It's been my first week as a waitress. I don't think Uncle Roger likes having me in the kitchen—it gets rowdy in there with all those guys. I don't mind, though." Her death grip on her glass relaxed a little.

"How old are you?"

"Twenty-one."

"So, about the ghost…"

"Yeah, you know I've never believed in this spirit stuff. My friend Jessica does, and I've gone along with it, mostly to make her happy. I mean, it's so important to her, and you should encourage your friends in what they feel passionate about, right?" She didn't wait for an answer. "But then working at the restaurant made me wonder. There was something creepy in the air, and things happened you couldn't explain. I saw with my own eyes a pot of boiling water jumping off the stove. Jeremy would've gotten scalded badly if he hadn't moved away just in time. He quit the next day. It made me change my mind about things."

"Have there been any incidents since the cleansing?"

"No! Not a single one. It smelled funny for a few days, that's all. The place even feels different, you can tell. Uncle Roger's happy as a clam. But then this thing happened with Jess, and I didn't know what to do. When you came to the restaurant, I knew it was a sign—you can help." She addressed just Denton now.

A barely audible groan from Denton's right informed him that Bran was nearing the limits of his endurance. Better get to the point. "Your friend, Jessica has trouble with a haunting, correct?"

She bobbed her head, and her locks bounced around her face. "She's possessed."

"Possessed?" That was the last thing he'd expected to hear.

"Yes."

"Isn't exorcism the area of the Catholic church?"

"I thought of it, but then I imagined the face of Father McKinley if I told him about Jess being taken over by an evil spirit. He'd think I was crazy. And Jess isn't like Linda Blair in that old movie. But if Mr. Maurell could chase a spirit out of a restaurant, he should be able to do it from a person. It's the same general principle, isn't it?" She sneaked a look at Bran.

After his silence, Bran's serious baritone startled Denton. "Maybe. Tell me what happened to your friend. From the beginning."

She pulled herself up straight and took a deep breath. "Jess and I have been friends since we were little. She saw a movie when she was seven and decided to become a witch. I wanted to be a ballerina at that age, but it passed. Jess, though, she stuck with it. It became her *thing*. She was doing tarot card readings and love spells by junior high. You know, I think it made her feel special. Everyone needs that sometime, and she sure didn't get it from her mother. Mrs. Porter ignored Jess most of the time, and when she didn't, it was only to let Jess know how disappointed she was in Jess. Or blame her for Mr. Porter leaving." Ashley's face darkened. "She wasn't a nice person. And you know, Jess has always been an average kid, not pretty or smart, but this witchery stuff made her feel special. She's a friend, and it makes her happy, so why not, right?" Ashley stopped and gave a weak smile as if she was trying to apologize for her friend.

Denton expected Bran to lose his patience, but he simply nodded. "Go on."

Ashley took a deep breath. "Okay, so Jess works as a psychic. Well, it's a part-time gig—she lives with her boyfriend, who has a good job, but she's talking about getting a little storefront somewhere. Right now she has a website, does house calls and stuff. Three weeks ago, she had an appointment for a séance. I went with her as I sometimes do. It was at a condo at Lincoln Square. A couple had just bought it, and they thought it was haunted. Or I think the wife thought so. She looked like the twitchy type, if you know what I mean. I think her husband went along with whatever she wanted. So, we started with an Ouija board to see if there was a presence. It's the way Jess likes to do it. It spelled *Nina*, and we all got excited. We started a regular séance, and Jess asked this Nina person to reveal herself."

"How?" Bran asked.

"What do you mean?"

"Were you sitting? Did you hold hands?"

"Oh, that. Yes. Of course. We sat around the dining room table, holding hands. A single white candle burned in the middle of the table."

"So you were part of the circle too?"

"Yeah. It was just the four of us. If it had been a bigger group, I would've stayed out."

"What happened next?"

"Not much at first, but then I felt this chill. I've done these things with Jess since we were twelve, but I've never felt anything like this before. The hair on my arms stood up. Then I think I saw something."

"What?"

"It's hard to tell, a shape or something. The room was dark with only the candle giving light, and I felt it more than I saw it. I thought maybe I was imagining it, but it freaked me out. Then the candle went out, and Jess started talking."

"What did she say?"

"Stuff like, *'No I don't want you. Go away. Leave me alone'*. Said *'no'* a lot of times. Then she got quiet. She seemed to have snapped out of it—shook herself and apologized. She said the spirit didn't want to communicate, but there was nothing to worry about. We left, but on the way home, I realized something was wrong."

"Wrong how?"

"I…it's hard to put into words. Jess wasn't herself. I thought maybe she was tired, but she's been this way since. As if she had a personality replacement, you know? Normally, she's quirky. She gets jealous of people, but she's never been mean. Now she's like someone on reality TV. Mean and bitchy, and she scares me."

"It's not exactly proof," Bran said.

"And I think she killed the neighbor's cat!"

Denton heard a throaty growl and realized it came from Murry.

Bran reached up stroked the cat. "You think?"

"There's a stuffed ginger tabby on her windowsill. She said she'd gotten it from an antique store, but there are missing cat posters all over the neighborhood, and the photo looks just like it."

"Hm."

She clutched her glass, and desperation filled her voice to the brim. "You have to believe me. There's something evil inside her. I'm afraid she'll do something really bad if we don't get rid of it." Her eyes flickered from one of them to the other, imploring. "I tried to find out who Nina was, but didn't have much luck. I have a list of everyone who lived in the apartment since 1936, but none of them is called Nina."

Bran's brows twitched up. "You have a list?"

She put the glass of water down on the table so fast it nearly tipped over. She caught it in time, and her face flushed red. "Sorry." She pulled a piece of paper out of her purse and handed it to Bran. "It's not a long list. The building used to be apartments, then co-op, and finally converted to condos two years ago. The last person living there before the current couple was a man named Michael Smith. There was a couple before him, Walter and Dee Manning, no children, and before them a woman named Esther Bernal. She lived there from the thirties till she died twelve years ago."

Denton peeked at the list—under the address stood the names and dates. Murry yawned and stretched and then jumped to the ground. He wound himself around Ashley's feet. She reached down and scratched his head. "Maybe Nina never lived there. A lot of things could've happened in the apartment in seventy years," she said. "She could've been, I dunno…maybe, you know, *murdered* there or something." She stared at them with eyes big and full of hope and pleading.

Bran folded up the sheet. "Maybe."

"So will you do it? I can pay. I have money saved up, and I can borrow from Uncle Roger if I have to."

Bran tapped his palm with the edge of the paper. "We'll talk about money later. I need to evaluate your friend first to be sure she's really possessed."

Even her freckles seemed to glow as she smiled. "Do you need to talk to her?"

"No. I want to observe her without her knowing."

"It's doable. We're going out on Friday night. Some place Jess picked—Club 9. Do you know where it is?"

"Yes."

"Oh, okay. We're supposed to be there around ten, but Jess is always late, so I guess we'll get there by eleven or so."

"Good. It's settled, then."

After thanking them profusely, she left. Bran saw her to the door and locked it behind her. It was time for Denton to leave too, but he had a few questions first.

Murry had something to say too. "Meow?"

Bran looked at the cat as if he understood. "I know. Dinner?"

"Meow!"

The two of them had this routine down pat. Denton could almost believe they were having an actual conversation. It was dorky cute, a lovable chink in Bran's armor of solemnity.

Denton followed them into the kitchen and watched Bran dump a can of cat food into a bowl, and Murry fell on it with gusto.

"Do you really think the girl might be possessed?" Denton asked, leaning on the doorjamb. Effectively, he had Bran cornered, and he liked the situation.

Bran stuck to his spot by the counter. "It's not impossible."

"Does it happen often?"

"Fortunately, no."

"Have you ever exorcised anyone?" Denton detached himself from the doorway and took a step inside.

Bran seemed to watch him with alarm. "No. And I'm not sure I can."

"Than what's the point of getting involved at all?" Denton took another step closer to his quarry.

Bran blinked and looked away. "Sometimes you just can't help yourself. Sorry, I must do some research into spirit possessions." He stepped around Denton and fled the kitchen.

"Fine! I'll just let myself out," Denton shouted after him.

Something bumped his leg, and he looked down to see Murry rubbing against him. "Your human is a real pill, you know."

"Meowrrr."

***

Friday night, Club 9 was hopping. Seasonal decorations of orange garlands and fluorescent skeletons alluded to the fact Halloween was only days away. The crowed seemed in a festive mood too—costumes and glitter competed for attention everywhere the eye could see. Denton had done his best on short notice to fit in. With generous amounts of gel, he'd shaped his hair into artful spikes. His ripped black jeans and white shirt emphasized his bony body. He'd added combat boots and a few chains for the full punk-rocker effect. Dark makeup around his eyes and on his lips made him come across downright eerie. At least he thought so.

Bran, on the other hand, had dressed in his usual head-to-toe black ensemble. With the long black trench coat, he had a sinister air, but it failed to impress Denton. "You could've made an effort."

Bran frowned at him, took tiara-style devil horns out of his satchel, snapped the cheap, plastic thing on his head, and glared back at Denton. "Happy?"

"No. Not really. Is this the best you can do?"

"Yes. What are you supposed to be, anyway?"

Denton shot him an indignant glare. "The ghost of Sid Vicious, of course. You know, if you were serious about it, you could rock the devil look. You have the physique for it. Some red body paint, tight leather pants…" The images he'd conjured burned bright in his mind's eyes. "Even better, assless chaps!" He joked, of course, about the chaps. Mostly. Although, he would've loved to get a glimpse of those buttocks at last. He grinned like mad.

Knots of consternation formed between Bran's brows. "Right. Let's find Ashley."

Killjoy. Trying to get Bran to have fun was like pulling teeth. "I should've dressed as a dentist," Denton grumbled to himself while trying to catch up to Bran, who had already taken off to search the crowd.

In the end, settling close to the bar turned out to be the best solution. As in the Serengeti, in a nightclub too, every beast returned to the watering hole sooner or later.

Denton noticed their quarry first. He nudged Bran. "There. Hermione Granger talking to the barman; that's Ashley."

Bran followed his gaze. "And the girl next to her must be Jessica. What is she dressed as?"

"Hm, I'm guessing slutty nurse. Very slutty."

The brunette Denton saw didn't fit the plain-Jane image he'd had of her after listening to Ashley. Sure, the girl wasn't a looker, but she had youth on her side. She would've been fine if she didn't appear so desperate for attention. The difference between the two girls was striking. Ashley had natural charm even in her fairly demure costume. She was attractive without trying, and all the straight guys noticed it. Meanwhile, Jessica, in her too-tight, too-short costume, functioned as a creep-magnet.

If he didn't know better, he would've mistaken Bran for one of those creeps. Bran watched Jessica like a hawk. He watched as she downed a red cocktail—Cosmopolitan, probably. He watched as she dashed to the dance floor, dragging Ashley with her, as she zapped to the bar, lustrous with sweat, had another Cosmo, and went back to dancing. Bran watched Jessica flirting without finesse with any guy straying into her orbit. He even watched as she and a swarthy zombie slipped away with the subtlety of a pair of elephants.

Ashley turned back from the bar with fresh drinks. Confusion spread over her expression as she couldn't see her friend. Bran waved to get her attention. She took another scan over the crowd before striding up to them.

"I'm so glad you're here. Did you see where Jess went?" Worry surrounded her like a thick coat.

Bran motioned toward the back door. "In the alley with some guy. We have a few minutes."

Her face fell. Hard. "I can't believe she'd do this. She loves Robbie. Jessica wouldn't cheat on him. This Nina bitch has taken control of her. Do you believe me now?"

She seemed on the edge of tears, so Denton patted her arm. "Don't worry. We'll take care of it. Right, Bran?"

"Right."

Ashley pulled herself together and nodded. "I better go before she sees us together. Thank you."

"So what's the verdict, is Jessica possessed?" Denton asked as Ashley scurried away.

"I'm still not absolutely sure. I have to get closer."

"I thought you were an expert."

"Possessions are rare and not easy to catch. My expertise is herbs, okay?"

"Fine! Don't bite my head off."

They waited. Jessica returned twenty minutes later, disheveled and misbuttoned. They couldn't hear the exchange between the two girls, but Ashley's anxiety and Jessica's disdain of it were easy to read. With a petulant air, Jessica turned her back to Ashley and marched to the bar. Ashley gave Denton and Bran a frustrated glance and followed her friend.

Bran tugged at the lapel of his coat. "I better do this now before they leave. Stay here." He too walked to the bar and wedged himself next to Jessica. He behaved the same as any other patron trying to attract the attention of the busy bartenders, but he also gave Jessica the once-over.

From his spot, Denton had a perfect view of what happened next. Jessica turned toward Bran with a coy smile on her lips, but her expression warped into a mix of fear and hatred. For a flicker, her features weren't even her own—Denton clearly saw the features of a strange woman snarling at Bran. Unfortunately, the bartender chose that moment to get to Bran, distracting him.

Denton could hardly believe his eyes as the tall glass in Jessica's hand smashed against the edge of the bar. Bran heard the sound of the glass breaking. He turned just in time to block the jagged edge of the glass aimed at his face. He stepped back, but she lunged at him again, with a low swing this time.

The attack happened so fast and out of the blue, everyone in the vicinity stood and stared in stunned silence. Soon, though, a couple of beefy bouncers rushed to the scene, along with Denton. One of them held a shrieking and struggling Jessica. The other had Bran's arm in a vise grip. A quick exchange between the bouncers and the barman cleared Bran of any wrongdoing, and the bouncer let him go. Bran announced he was fine and didn't need medical attention. It seemed to satisfy the two men, who proceeded to eject Jessica from the club. A mortified Ashley followed her.

Bran pulled his coat tightly around himself and shoved his hands into its pockets. "We should go."

Chapter Three

In the cab rushing them back home, Denton was still processing the events. "Did you expect her to do that?" He kept his voice low, although the cabbie paid no attention to them.

"No, of course not. I don't know what made her flip."

Denton sniffed, had a flashback of the time he and Bran ran into each other in front of their building, then sniffed again. "What was the last time you got your coat dry-cleaned?"

"What?"

"It reeks of burned sage. You're probably too used to it to notice, but the *doorman* at our building gets agitated when you get close. I bet it's the smell." He didn't say he meant the *ghostly* doorman, but he didn't have to.

"Oh. I didn't think of that." Bran leaned back and closed his eyes.

Denton took the opportunity to study him up close. Something more than just fatigue etched lines on Bran's face. Denton got the distinct impression he was seeing a man who kept his façade in place by force of will. Powers of observation weren't Denton's strength, so this slip of intuition came as a surprise. Driven by instinct, he reached for Bran's hand and gave it a squeeze. Bran rolled his head sideways, and a half smile softened his expression. He squeezed back.

Denton felt stickiness under his fingers. He looked closer. It was blood. "You're hurt! We should go to the emergency room."

Bran pulled his hand away, and his features hardened into the haughty mask he used to keep the world away.

Denton gritted his teeth in frustration. He didn't say a word, but he thought of many. By the time the cab dropped them at the Balmoral, he'd worked himself into a seething ball of fury, ready to blow. If Bran thought Denton would simply stand by, batting his eyes like some damsel in a stupid romance novel, he had another fucking thing coming.

His opening came at their floor. Stepping out of the elevator, Bran reached into his pocket for his keys, and his coat fell open.

Denton noticed for the first time the large rip in Bran's jeans over his left thigh. "What's that?"

"Nothing." Bran bolted to his door, key in hand.

Denton wasn't about to let him go so easy. "Nothing, my ass. She cut you, didn't she?"

"It's just a scratch." Bran opened the door and stepped inside.

Denton slapped his hand on the door before Bran could shut him out, and pushed inside. "Bullshit!" He grabbed Bran by the elbow and pulled him into the living room, flipping every light switch on as they went. "Stay still. I'm going to look at this *scratch*, and if it's worse than you say, I'll drag you to the ER, even if I have to knock you unconscious first. I said stay still!" he snapped at Bran, who tried to pull away.

Denton dropped to his knees in front of Bran. The tattered gash in the fabric turned out to be bigger than he'd first thought. It hardly seemed possible that an ordinary girl like Jessica could do so much damage. It had to be the spirit inside her. The denim under Denton's fingers was damp with blood. The blackness of the jeans had disguised it. And, of course, Bran had done his best to hide it. *Stupid idiot.*

"Take your pants off," Denton commanded.

"What? No!"

Bran moved to step away, but Denton grabbed him behind both knees. He had no patience left for these games. He held on to Bran and turned his face up to give Bran the benefit of his pissed-off glare. He knew if it was physically possible, lightning would've shot from his eyes. He kept his voice even, but the words clipped together like links in a chain. "Take your fucking jeans off. I've already seen your package. No surprises there. I don't know what the hell your problem is, but get over it."

Bran stood statue-still. His eyes, wide and fixed on Denton's, were deeper and more unfathomable than night. His hands drifted to his belt, and seconds later, the jeans dropped around his ankles. Satisfied with his small victory, Denton turned his attention back to the injury, which left him dumbfounded. Amid half-dried blood, a jagged white scar stood out, but it couldn't possibly have been a fresh wound. It made no sense—there was no other cut, but the blood must've come from somewhere. He traced his fingers over the puckered skin running halfway around Bran's thigh.

As he shifted, something else caught his eye. "What the…" He moved more for a better view. And there it was: an appendage, which could only be described as a tail, because that was what it was—long and smooth, hairless except for fine fuzz. Strange as it was, it fit—the skin had the same olive tone as the rest of Bran's body, and the way the tail had grown, it seemed a natural continuation of his coccyx. Even hanging limp, the tail was sleek and elegant. It complemented the muscular globes of his buttocks.

"I stand corrected—this is a surprise," Denton murmured.

He had to touch it. He put his fingers on the thick base and slid them down the evenly thinning length of twelve or so inches, to the blunt tip. It felt warm and firm. Only then did he notice the tremors racing through Bran's body. He snatched his hand away. "Sorry, does it hurt? I didn't think…"

Bran shook his head but said nothing. He'd firmly shut his eyes in the manner of a man who was too afraid to look. He appeared outright frightened, and it confused Denton. Then a lightbulb in his head turned on at last. Having an extra body part would inhibit most men, but for someone as introverted as Bran, it had to be a curse.

Denton stood up and moved around to be face-to-face with Bran. He stepped in till they were chest-to-chest and put his arms around Bran's waist. At the moment of contact, Bran sunk into Denton's embrace, burying his face in Denton's shoulder. Denton rubbed his hand over Bran's back with a shushing motion. Bran hung on to him tightly.

"Hey." Denton patted him. "It's okay. So you have a tail. No biggie."

"No?" Bran's asked hoarsely.

"Nah. It's rather sexy, if you ask me."

A choked laugh shook Bran. He leaned back and finally met Denton's eyes. "There's something I have to tell you."

Denton pursed his lips. "You got the order of things all mixed up. We're past that part."

"Let me finish."

"Fine. Go on."

Bran took a deep breath. "I'm half demon."

Denton half disbelieved him. "Like Hell Boy?"

Bran sighed with exasperation, but it showed him starting to unwind. "Hell Boy is full demon, and a comic book character. I'm serious. My father is an honest-to-goodness demon."

Denton thought about it for a moment and came to the conclusion he wasn't bothered. "Okay."

Obviously, it wasn't the answer Bran had expected. "Okay? Is that it?"

"You're talking to a man who sees dead people. So you're the son of a demon. Poor excuse for being such a secretive, unsociable jerk, in my opinion." Okay, Denton still harbored a trace of irritation.

Bran cleared his throat. "Umm. I take full credit for being a jerk."

"I'm sure the tail didn't help. C'mon, let's get you in the shower. You're a bloody mess, and I'm not just saying it to sound British." Denton wanted to slide his hands to Bran's buttocks and give them a hearty squeeze, but he figured it might come across as insensitive under the circumstances.

***

Having pushed Bran under the spray of water, Denton stripped his own clothing and stepped in after him. Bran neither objected nor commented. His demeanor was subdued, and it worried Denton, but his instincts told him to simply be there. For the first time being together fully naked, the shower was a chaste affair. Seeing Bran in the nude got Denton excited, but then he felt like a heel for thinking about sex when Bran had his mind on other things. The guilt took over and thumped his lust.

Once they were clean and dry, towels wrapped around their waists, they tottered off to the bedroom. Bran slipped under the blanket, and Denton got ready to tuck him in as a dutiful caretaker. Bran must have had other ideas, because he grabbed Denton's wrist and pulled him into the cocoon of the blanket. Denton had no desire to resist.

Bran radiated heat like a furnace under the blanket. Denton pressed his hand on Bran's naked skin. "You have a fever."

Bran joggled his head sideways. "My normal body temperature is two degrees higher than anybody else's."

"Well, I thought you were hot before but didn't realize you were literally," Denton joked. They hadn't had much physical closeness aside from quick sex, and on those occasions, he'd been too distracted. Heat of passion and stuff.

He wouldn't be rushed this time. Bran didn't seem to be in a hurry either, for a change. He mapped Denton's lean body with his hands. He showed distinct interest in Denton's piercings. He kept touching and tweaking the silver ring decorating Denton's left nipple, observing the corresponding shudders running through Denton with curious wonder.

"You like this?" Bran asked.

"Can't you tell?"

"Doesn't it hurt?"

In response, Denton bent his head over Bran's chest and scraped his teeth over a nipple. He followed it up with gentler caresses with his tongue and lips. Bran gasped, and his body grew taut. His chest rose and fell in a slow and heavy pace.

Denton peppered kisses across Bran's chest and down his sternum, then his abdomen next, sliding deeper under the blanket as he went. Bran had a dark pelt of hair over his pecs in the shape of a bird with outstretched wings. His stomach, on the other hand, stretched as a hair-free expanse, broken only by the narrow strip of the treasure trail, which Denton followed all the way to the hem of the towel.

He didn't untuck it right away but instead rubbed his face on the bulge of Bran's cock through the fabric. He tugged the towel loose little by little. When Bran's shaft emerged, Denton licked the shiny head. As he turned his attention to Bran's sac, he noticed the tail tucked under Bran's thigh. He coaxed it out and put a kiss on the end, then pressed and glided his tongue along the appendage as far as he could. The muffled moan coming from the direction of the head of the bed told him he was on the right track. He settled between Bran's spread legs and proceeded to give the best blowjob of his life.

Denton felt the tail under him—he was careful not to crush it—twitching in response to what he was doing. Then it curled up, slipped along Denton's chest, and the tip prodded his left nipple, the one with the ring. The touch was surprisingly deft, almost the same as a finger. When Bran climaxed, the tail tensed and relaxed as the rest of him did.

After catching his breath, Bran reversed their positions. He made an effort to draw out the experience, but Denton was too keyed up to last.

They lay in languid silence for a good while. With his head on Bran's chest, listening to the unhurried thump-thump of Bran's heart, Denton dozed off. Bran's shuffling around woke him.

"Mmm… What's it?" he asked sleepily.

"Shh, nothing. I'm just trying to get rid of the towel. Lift your hip a bit."

Denton did, and the terrycloth slipped from under him. They rearranged themselves, Bran on his back, Denton tucked in the crook of his arm.

"Go back to sleep," Bran said, but it was too late. Denton was wide awake.

Stray thoughts kept running around his head, keeping the sandman away. "What does your father look like?" he asked.

Bran took his time to answer. Sharing intimate details of his life had to be a new experience, needing consideration. "Not pretty. Grotesque by human standards. Horns, tail, scales, fur."

"How did your mom… I mean…"

"End up having sex with him?"

"Well, yeah." Denton felt himself flush. Talking about mothers and sex in the same breath felt wrong.

"Demons are tricksters and shape changers. They can appear in human form. Although there's always something to give them away. For my dad, it's the feet."

"What do you mean?"

"Cloven as a goat's."

Denton had no intent to speak ill of Denton's mother. "I guess under the right circumstances, unusual feet can go unnoticed."

He'd meant to sound conciliatory, but Bran snorted. "Between the two of us, I'm convinced my father was the one tricked. You don't know my mother. She gives a new meaning to the word *devious*, and my dad's not the worldliest demon in the pack. He's more of a scholar."

Denton took a good minute to wrap his head around this information, especially the scholar-demon part, but something else piqued his curiosity more.

"No offense, but why would your mom want to seduce a demon?"

Bran heaved a sigh. "Because mothers want the best for their offspring. Mine's simply crazier than most. She speculated that combining her witch genes with a demon's would produce an exceptionally talented child. Instead, all I inherited from him was a tail and quick healing. At least the latter is useful."

"She sounds…interesting." More like nutty, Denton thought, but he didn't want to judge.

"Despite her strange ways, she's been a typical mother. Protective, meddling, and loving. She homeschooled me till I was twelve. By then I knew how to hide my tail from everyone."

"So, basically you've been hiding your tail from everyone all this time? Didn't you ever have the urge to share it with someone you were close to?"

Bran's face drained of expression. "I did once, when I was young, but it didn't turn out well at all. I haven't let myself get close enough to anyone to want to since."

"And now?"

Bran took in a shuddering breath and turned to his side, winding his limbs around Denton. "Tell me it's not a mistake," he whispered into Denton's skin.

"It's not." Denton burrowed himself into Bran's embrace and fell asleep.

Chapter Four

Denton woke tangled up in sheets and lying across the bed all by himself. Well, not entirely. Murry sat next to him, Day-Glo eyes fixed on his face.

"Morning, kitty," Denton said and stretched his hand toward the cat.

With a hiss, Murry evaded him and hopped to the floor.

"He doesn't like being called cute names." Bran stood in the door, wearing his cranberry-red bathrobe. In his hand, he held a large cup. Bittersweet scent teased Denton's nostrils.

"Is that coffee? More importantly, is it for me?"

"Yes and yes." Bran walked up and handed over the cup. "It's the way you like it: sickly sweet."

"You're a sexy man." Denton took a grateful swallow of his coffee. It was just sweet enough.

Bran turned, but Denton grabbed the edge of the bathrobe with his free hand and pulled Bran back. "How're you feeling?"

Looking down, Bran tilted his head and smiled—a real, visible, recognizable-by-anyone smile. "Good. You?"

"More than. Come back to bed." Denton blindly reached back toward the night table till he heard the cup safely clop down onto it. Then he used both hands to haul Bran closer. Bran gave in and dropped onto the edge of the bed. He pulled Denton in for a kiss. He tasted like toothpaste— sexy, minty toothpaste. Denton tugged at the rope holding the robe closed.

"You're worse than an incubus," Bran said, but he pushed Denton back on the bed and slipped his hand under the covers.

Loud buzzing from the direction of the left pocket of Bran's robe interrupted them. Bran pulled the phone out and squinted at the screen. "Sorry, I have to take this. It's David from the Historical Society." He sat up straight. "David? … You did? That was fast. … It is?" With visible excitement, but not the sexual kind, he stood and dashed out of the room.

Denton knew when he was beat. He rolled off the bed and, taking his coffee with him, headed off in the direction of the bathroom. When he returned twenty minutes or so later, clean and caffeinated, he found the bedroom empty. The cranberry-red bathrobe lay across the bed. Denton didn't want to put on his dirty clothes from the day before, so he took the robe. It smelled of Bran. He found the man in question in his study—a repurposed second bedroom.

He'd only had glimpses of this inner sanctum of Bran's, so he took in the view from the doorway. Overflowing bookshelves took up one corner, a desk with computer, scanner, and printer another. Two big cork boards covered the available wall space. They were covered in several layers of paper—pictures of plants, photocopies of printed articles, handwritten notes, a calendar, and more. And of course, potted plants crowded the windowsills.

Bran sat in the middle of it, tapping away at the keyboard. He seemed at home in the middle of this creative chaos. He heard Denton stepping in, and he turned around.

"You found out something, I can tell. Out with it," Denton said.

Bran made an unsuccessful effort to hide his self-satisfaction. "Okay. Here it is: there's no tilde on Ouija boards."

"Who's Tilde?"

"Not who. What. The accent over the letter 'n' in some Spanish words."

"O-kay. I believe you. So?"

"There's no Nina. The spirit spelled niña—child in Spanish."

Denton liked Bran this way—enthusiastic and relaxed. "Have I told you how handsome you are when you're smug?"

"Be serious."

"I am. Okay, go on. Prove to me why the board spelled niña. I know you want to."

"Right. I asked David to see if the Historical Society had anything on any of the previous occupants of the apartment. It turns out I could've Googled it." Bran triumphantly pulled a sheet of paper out of the printer and handed it to Denton.

It was a newspaper article from three years earlier. Denton quickly scanned it. The mummified body of a newborn had been found in an old trunk in the basement of the apartment building. The building manager, cleaning out a long-unused storage space, came upon the trunk and pried it open. He found old magazines, photographs, and letters addressed to one Esther Bernal. He also came across a green bowl and the skeletal remains of a newborn wrapped in a scarf and newspaper dated 1942. The manager immediately notified the police, who took the body and some of the documents but left the bowl.

"Wow." Denton looked from the printout to Bran. "So the baby's probably Esther's. How old would she've been in forty-two?"

"Twenty. There's more. Bernal's not a common name, and David thought he'd heard it before. He dug in and found something. Alfonso Bernal fled from Spain in 1937 with his daughter, Esther, to escape fascism. He enjoyed popularity in the forties as a portrait painter for Chicago's well-to-do, till his death in nineteen fifty."

"How did he die?"

"Fell off the balcony of his apartment while drunk."

Denton moved closer and parked his butt on the edge of Bran's desk. He could think better sitting down. "So Alfonso had to be involved in the hiding and probably the death of the baby."

"It stands to reason."

"But why would either of them do it? Do you think…" Unpleasant notions of incest and rape ran through Denton's head, but he didn't want to give them shape by saying them out loud.

The wrinkle on Bran's forehead suggested he had to have notions of the same, but he didn't want to give them a name either. "I don't think we'll ever know. Esther died in 2002 at age eighty. It's doubtful we'd find anyone to tell us what she might have done sixty years ago."

"And she'd probably kept the baby secret from everyone, anyway."

"Something very ugly had to have happen to her, though, for her spirit to stick around and be strong enough to possess a person after all this time."

Denton remembered something. "I think I saw her last night."

Bran perked up. "You did?"

"Just for a second, before she attacked you."

"What did she look like?"

Denton thought about it. "Sort of unremarkable but young, not an eighty-year-old woman. Is that normal?"

Bran knotted his brows and tapped his fingers to his lips. "I don't know—I can't see them. But if Esther had gotten emotionally stuck at a certain age, it sounds reasonable for her visual manifestation to reflect it. I think."

He looked so grimly handsome, Denton couldn't help but comment. "You're the only man I know who can say such things and sound completely scientific."

"Are you ever serious?"

"No. Are you ever not serious?"

Bran took Denton's hand in his own and held it palm up. With his fingers around Denton's wrist, he rubbed Denton's palm with his thumb. "I don't know. Maybe. I'll try."

There was so fucking much earnestness in those words, they slashed through Denton's heart with the precision of a surgical blade. He took Bran's face in his hands and kissed him gently on the lips. Bran returned the kiss with the kind of passion he hadn't shown before. Denton liked it. A lot.

"So what are we gonna do now?" Denton asked when they pulled apart.

Bran looked uncharacteristically uncertain. "Umm, stuff people do when they date?"

Denton felt a jolly grin taking over his face, but had to get back to the other matter at hand. "I'd like that, but I was thinking about Jessica. Can you exorcise her?"

Bran took a deep breath and let it out. "Oh, that. No, I don't have the skills. I could end up hurting her."

"So is this it? We do nothing?" Denton couldn't believe Bran would give up so easily.

Bran wouldn't. "I have an idea."

"Oh for goodness sake, don't make me get the thumb screws. Tell me already." *One of these days I am gonna strangle this man.*

"Instead of trying to drive out Esther's spirit, I will summon it."

"So it leaves Jessica's body?" Denton was catching on.

"Exactly. Sunday's All Hallows Eve. An auspicious time for witchcraft."

"Okay, you summon her. Then what?"

"Then you banish it as you did Vinnie Pagano."

Denton didn't feel as confident about this part as Bran seemed to be. "What if I can't?"

"You will," Bran said without a hint of doubt.

"You have way too much faith in my abilities."

"I have faith in you."

Well, shit. Denton was touched, more than he could say, so he kept his trap shut.

Bran kept talking. "I've talked to Ashley. She believes we could schedule Jessica for a séance if we offered her enough money. But we have a problem—we need somebody she hasn't seen yet who would let us use their apartment. I don't know many people who'd do that, especially on such short notice."

Denton knew just the person. "I do. He owes me a couple of favors. Let me make a call."

He dialed his friend Gabe and explained the situation in bold strokes. Gabe agreed without much fuss—the man had an admirable aptitude for going with the flow. Also, as a former vampire hunter now in the employ of Chicago's top vamp, he was used to the extraordinary. The perfect person for the situation.

"It's all settled." Denton snapped his phone closed and grinned. "Now what?"

He hoped for some frivolity, but to his misfortune, Bran's mind was on the job already. "I have a lot of preparations to make, and you absolutely need to practice."

A sigh left Denton in a disappointed whoosh. "Oh fine, I'll practice. Tell me one last thing. Is Jessica a witch the same as you are?"

"Not at all. She doesn't have a single witchy bone in her body."

Denton started at him in confusion. "How can you say that? She summoned a spirit."

"No, she didn't. Ashley did."

"What?"

"She doesn't know it, but she has the talent. It's plain bad luck she was part of a séance at a place with such a hungry spirit."

Denton still didn't get it. "But then why did it possess Jessica and not Ashley?"

"Ashley served as the medium to summon her, but Jessica had the weakness making her suitable for possession. You didn't think a spirit could take over anyone willy-nilly, did you?"

"I…I don't know what I thought."

"Good. I need to make a call to my mother. If anyone can help me form a plan, it's her. Practice?"

"Fine, fine."

***

They spent the next day and a half in a flurry of preparations. They met with Ashley, and Bran explained to her how it was the spirit of Esther Bernal possessing Jessica's body but said nothing about Ashley's role in the matter. They concocted a plan to lure Jessica to Gabe's apartment for a Halloween-night séance. Ashley would introduce Gabe as a friend of her parents to avert suspicion. A large fee to be paid to Jessica for such a last-minute arrangement would serve as an additional enticement.

Halloween night found Bran and Denton in Bran's car, parked a block from the apartment Gabe shared with his vampire boyfriend, Harvey. Those two were an interesting couple, especially since Gabe was a reformed slayer. An inauspicious pairing, yet they made it work. It gave Denton hope, made him believe he and Bran had a chance.

He hadn't told Bran about Harvey being undead, because he didn't think it was his secret to share. Anyway, Harvey might not even be there tonight. Denton made his arrangements with Gabe only. Maybe he should test the waters, just in case.

"How do you feel about vampires?" he asked conversationally.

Bran didn't even look up from the dusty old tome he'd had his nose in all day. "I don't bother them if they don't bother me."

"Live and let unlive?"

"Right." Bran flipped a page and traced the lines of text with his fingers.

Denton couldn't be entirely sure if Bran had been serious or humoring him, or if he'd even heard a word Denton said. Oh well, he'd tried. There was no use making small talk with Bran when he got this preoccupied.

Denton's phone rang, and he answered it. He listened to Gabe's update and relayed it to Bran. "Gabe's got Jessica secured in the apartment. It's time for us to show up."

They approached the basement apartment from the alley. Gabe opened the door. He looked Bran over with sharp, assessing eyes. Denton had once had an interest in Gabe, before he'd known about Harvey, and it was easy to remember why. Dark-haired, and well-built, Gabe reminded Denton of a predator—he had the coiled power of a hunter. Denton resisted the urge to compare the two men, but watching them side by side, he saw the similarities. Bran's strength was less obvious, but it went deeper.

Bran wore the same aloof air he had when Denton first met him. By now, Denton recognized it as Bran's way of dealing with being out of his comfort zone, which was pretty much all the time around strangers.

After brief introductions, they moved into the living room, where Jessica lay on the sofa, arms and legs bound. Thick ropes coiled around her body and the seat of the sofa so she couldn't roll off. She glared at everyone but said nothing. Silver duct tape covered her mouth.

"She tried to bite," Gabe explained.

Ashley, who kneeled on the floor next to her friend, stopped chewing her fingernails for a second. "It wasn't really her." Ashley was a mess. Her mascara was smeared, and her hair hung in a frazzled lump.

"True," agreed Bran, taking a jar out of his satchel. He dipped his index finger into the sticky brown goo and used it to draw a pentagram on Jessica's forehead. Next he produced a large white seashell, which he placed on the side table by Jessica's head, put a cone of incense into the shell, and lit it. He followed it up with simply crouching there, eyes closed and head bent. Denton guessed Bran was centering himself, so he waited.

Gabe demonstrated less patience. "Can we get this hocus-pocus on the road already?"

Bran straightened up and shot a narrow-eyed glare at Gabe.

Before he could say anything, Harvey walked into the room. "What's that smell?"

All heads turned toward him. Denton caught a glimpse of adoration in Gabe's eyes. He had to admit, Harvey looked good—in a slender, dark-eyed, fine-featured way. Part Chinese to boot, for an exotic flare. Hot. If you were into that sort of thing.

Clearly, Bran wasn't, because he accosted Harvey straight away. "What are you doing here?"

"This is my apartment," Harvey snapped back.

"You're wrong. You shouldn't be here," Bran insisted.

"What the hell do you mean *wrong*?" Harvey put his hands on his hips. For a small guy, he acted fierce, but that was easy for a vampire.

Denton jumped in before they could find out who'd win in a half-demon versus vampire fistfight. He produced his most affable smile. "What Bran means is, you're *different*, and while he sincerely appreciates you letting us use your apartment, it's throwing off his concentration. *Right, Bran?*" Denton turned to Bran, eyes semaphoring a warning message.

Bran blinked. "Right." Then, facing Harvey, he added, "My apologies."

Gabe strolled up, pulled Harvey close to him, and whispered something into his ear. The first time Gabe had mentioned Harvey to Denton, he'd called Harvey his "roommate," but the intimacy of the simple gesture spoke of much more. Under Gabe's caress, Harvey let go of his fight-ready posture.

"Fine," he said when Gabe stepped away. "I'll go. Call me when you're done." Then pointedly at Bran: "If you make a mess, you'd better clean it up. I won't scrub ectoplasm out of the carpet after you." Grabbing his cellphone, he stormed out.

Gabe made a WTF face at Denton, who could only shrug in reply. Who knew what would set off Mr. Bossy-pants?

Unaware of this exchange, Bran pulled several items out of his bag before stashing it out of the way. He also removed the tape covering Jess's mouth. She bared her teeth at him, but he kept out of biting range.

As Gabe and Denton watched him curiously—and even Ashley forgot about her fretting and turned in their direction—Bran laid a roughly two-foot-by-two-foot black silk cloth on the floor. He sprinkled ordinary powdered sugar on it in the shape of a triangle and within it a circle. Denton had been surprised to see the box among Bran's supplies earlier, but Bran assured him of sugar's unmatched summoning power. In the middle of the cloth, Bran placed a disk-shaped object. Denton peered closer and saw a large silver medallion of a pentagram enclosed in a circle, strange symbols engraved all around its circumference.

Bran placed three votive candles—a white, a black, and a red—at each corner of the triangle and lit them. He murmured a few words. The candles flickered once, and the lines of sugar connecting them started to emanate a faint glow.

Bran stood. "Okay, let's get on with this *hocus-pocus*."

Gabe straightened his face. "Fine. What do we do?"

Bran instructed them to stand around the cloth. Ashley took her place on Bran's right, Denton on his left, and Gabe across.

Bran stretched out his arms. "Hold the hands of the persons next to you." Then to Denton: "Relax your mind and focus, as we practiced."

Ashley fidgeted. "Should we think of something? Jess has always told me to concentrate on the spirit we want to summon. Should I concentrate on Esther?"

Bran stared at her as if she'd suggested something radical, then nodded. "Yes. You should do that."

"Me too?" asked Gabe.

Without sparing him a glance, Bran said, "Sure," and took Denton's and Ashley's hands.

Looking off into space, he began to chant in Spanish. The repetitive rise and fall of Bran's voice had a calming effect on Denton and helped him tune out his environment.

"*Puta!*" Jessica's shriek jolted Denton out if his concentration. He saw Ashley jump too. Bran squeezed Denton's hand, as he probably did Ashley's, and kept on repeating the same rhythmic phrases, as if nothing had happened. Denton got the message and did his best to ignore Jessica.

"You can't do this. This is kidnapping. You'll go to prison!" she kept shouting, but nobody responded to her. A string of curses followed and another threat. "Un-fucking-tie me, or I'll kill you all, like I killed the drunk bastard!"

When they ignored her, she kept cursing and throwing threats and expletives at them, but as she went on, fewer of her words were in English and more in Spanish.

To tune her out, Denton thought about the warmth of Bran's hand, the self-assured firmness that his touch conveyed. He let that sense of certainty take him over, and with it he felt light filling him up, ounce by ounce. Then there was quiet, and Denton opened his eyes—he'd only just realized he'd closed them—and saw a wisp of smoke rise in the space between them, twist and grow. It whirled with the momentum of a swarm of angry wasps, gaining volume in every spin, till it was the size and rough shape of a person. Denton thought he could see traces of an angry young woman, but it was hard to tell.

Bran gave Denton's hand another squeeze, then let him go. Denton knew what to do. He let go of Gabe and raised his hands, palms outward. A wave of heat washed through him and burst out of his hands in the form of bright white light. It engulfed the smoky form of Esther's spirit. A brief flash later, there was only empty space over the summoning circle.

Ashley stared at Denton with her jaw dropped, and even the seasoned Gabe seemed impressed. However, Bran's pleased expression made Denton the proudest.

He grinned back. "Say, 'It'll do, pig. It'll do.'"

Of course, he only managed to confuse Bran, who must not have seen *Babe* either. "Pig?"

"Never mind. I'll explain later."

Gabe was already untying an unconscious Jessica, while Ashley stood by, watching and tugging strands of her own hair.

"Is she okay?" she asked Gabe.

"I don't know. Harvey could tell if he was here. He used to be a nurse."

If Bran caught the bite in the comment, he didn't show it. He knelt next to the sofa. "Bring me a glass of water."

Ashley sprang to action and was back with a glass in seconds. Bran dipped a handkerchief into the water and used it to clean the pentagram off Jessica's forehead. He handed the glass back to Ashley. "Thank you."

Shoving the wet handkerchief into his pocket, he produced a small bottle. He unscrewed its top and held it under Jessica's nose.

Jessica jerked awake. "Hey! What? What's going on?" Her eyes flitted from one face to another, fear fighting with confusion.

Bran backed off, and Gabe took charge. He patted Jessica's hand. "How are you feeling? Are you all right?"

She turned her full attention to him. "I remember arriving. You were here, and another guy. None of these people, and then… I don't know. What happened?"

"We were having a séance, Jess, and the spirit took you over. You don't remember?" Ashley lied smoothly without batting an eye.

"No. Not a thing."

Ashley bit her lip. "You were taken over by the spirit, and then you passed out." Not an outright lie—Denton admired her quick thinking.

A touch of pride colored Jessica's cheeks. "It happens to us mediums sometimes," she said with perfect seriousness.

Ashley stoked the fire. "It was amazing! The spirit totally spoke through you."

"What did it say?"

"Well, eh, it was in Spanish, so we didn't understand any of it."

"Oh wow."

During this exchange Bran withdrew and quietly packed away all evidence of the night's activities. After all the drama, the night wound down without further commotion. Gabe offered to drive Jessica and Ashley home, which they took him up on. Ashley even gave him a flirty smile—barking up the wrong tree, poor girl.

***

They met with Ashley at Starbucks a couple of days later. Denton sipped his Caramel Macchiato with extra syrup while Bran looked on with scorn. "It's a caffeinated, liquid candy bar."

"I know! Isn't it great?"

Bran shook his head and turned to Ashley. "How's Jessica doing?"

"She's herself again, if that's what you're asking. She still can't remember anything after arriving at your friends' apartment. Her memories of the last several weeks are hazy."

"Does she have any idea she's been possessed?"

"No, and I haven't had the heart to tell her. Should I?"

The answer took its time coming. Finally, Bran shook his head. "No. She doesn't need to know." He produced a rectangular cardboard box from his bag and put it on the table between them. "Give this to her. Make sure she hangs it up somewhere at her place."

Ashley opened it a peeked inside. Denton craned his neck and got a glimpse of a colorful glass ball the size of a Christmas ornament.

"What is it?" Ashley asked.

"Witch ball to trap negative spirits."

"Oh. Thank you! Jessica will love it."

Bran nodded and picked up his own coffee—dark Sumatra, straight, no sugar.

Jessica put the box into her purse. "Umm. So, uh, how much do I owe you?"

"Five thousand dollars."

She flushed red and swallowed, while Denton nearly choked on his coffee.

Unfazed by their reactions, Bran went on. "But I waive my fee, if you promise me one thing."

With hopefulness in her eyes, Jessica perked up. "Sure! What?"

"Don't go helping Jessica with her witchy things again. Furthermore, don't ever go anywhere near a Ouija board. No tarot cards or anything even seeming close to witchcraft."

She brightened. "Oh, that'll be easy! This experience will last me a lifetime. If I never have to go through anything like this again, I'll die happy."

"Swear." Bran leaned forward, and his eyes bored into her.

"I swear!" said Ashley with complete seriousness. She even put a hand over her heart.

"Good. We're square, then." Bran leaned back in his chair.

While Bran looked on with disinterest, Denton and Ashley made small talk about the weather, the restaurant, and her future plans in the hospitality business. She bit her lip and gave him a speculative look. "Can I ask you something?"

"Shoot."

"Your friend, Gabe, is he single?"

"No, sorry. He and Harvey are an item."

She slapped her forehead. "Duh! I'm so stupid. How did I not see that? I mean I knew right away you two were a couple. You are, right?" she added with an anxious frown.

To Denton's surprise, Bran answered before he could. "Right."

"Phew. You two look like you belong together, you know?"

This had Denton baffled. He and Bran couldn't have looked less similar. "How?"

"Oh, I dunno, you just do. Like you complement each other. Like Rocky and Bullwinkle." With another blush, she grabbed her purse. "I should go before I make bigger ass of myself."

She stood, and, thanking them again profusely, she gave them both hugs and a kiss each on their cheeks.

"She's batty," Denton said when she was out the door.

"Nah, I don't think so," Bran replied.

"You could've told her she had the talent."

Bran shook his head. "She has plans for her life. Why ruin them?"

Denton had plans too, and they involved a certain half-demon witch. One of these days, he'd tell Bran about them.

DESOLATE SPIRIT

Chapter One

Bran stood in front of the bathroom sink, shaving. He wore a black jock strap and nothing else. The wide elastic bands framed his firm buttocks in the most aesthetically pleasing way—a view Denton could never get bored with. The lazy back and forth swing of Bran's tail signaled his good mood.

"You shouldn't wear anything else in the house," Denton said from his spot at the doorway.

"I can't run around practically naked. It wouldn't be proper," Bran replied to the mirror.

"Proper-schmopper. I hate those baggy jeans. So fugly. And isn't it uncomfortable shoving your tail into them?"

"I'm used to it."

"You could wear assless chaps, as I suggested before."

"No way."

Denton had more ideas. "How about a kilt? It would be comfortable yet respectable."

Before Bran could object again, Denton's phone intruded into the conversation.

Denton spied Joy's number on the screen. He lifted the phone to his ear, but Joy cut him off before he opened his mouth.

"Hey, ferret-face, are you awake? Is the computer on? I've got a job for us, but I need you to look at this website first." Her words gushed from the phone in a breathless torrent.

"Good morning to you too, Pumpkin. I can't look at the computer right now—I'm not at home."

Joy's shocked silence hung between them for a couple of seconds till she found her voice again. "Where on earth are you at eight thirty in the morning?"

"Next door."

"Oooh, spent the night with Mr. Dark and Mysterious? Nice. I hope he treats you right," she cooed.

Denton raised his voice to make sure Bran wouldn't miss a word. "Mr. Dark and Mysterious ravaged me last night. Three times."

KLUNK! Fortunately, the electric razor fell into the sink and not on the floor. It could've broken.

Denton returned Bran's vexed glare, making a kissy-face.

Joy's giggle tickled his ear. "More info than I needed to have, but I'm happy for you. Will there be an encore? Should I call back in an hour or two?"

"Nah, just give me a few minutes and I'll call you. Okay?"

After hanging up, Denton made his way to the bedroom to find his socks—his favorite lime-green pair. He located one right away, but the other one was hiding. He crouched and looked under the bed—spotting it right away. But that wasn't the only thing he noticed. He looked at Bran, who'd just walked into the room. "There's something under your bed."

"What do you mean, something?" Bran asked, pulling on his jeans.

"I dunno. Some stuff hanging from the underside of the frame."

Bran squatted down next to Denton and took a long look. "Whatta…" He stood. "Come, help me flip the mattress."

Denton did, although he clearly wasn't the muscle in the operation. Fortunately, Bran made up for Denton's lack of brawn. The procedure still took some heaving and grunting, which woke Murry's curiosity. The cat sat in the doorway and watched them with pie-eyed interest.

They stood the mattress on its side, propped against the wall. Its underside held a surprise—a large drawing of what looked like a plus sign, with straight and curvy lines crossing all four of its legs in an asymmetric pattern.

Bran furrowed his brow but said nothing. He turned his attention to the bed frame and untied the string holding the thing Denton had spotted earlier. It turned out to be two crude human figures, six or so inches long and made out of twigs and torn cloth. Denton couldn't fail to notice the strategically placed sticks that made them both male. Oh, and they both had the same symbol drawn on them: an upside-down triangle with straight lines attached to it.

Bran rubbed the pieces of cloth between his fingers. "So that's where that dirty sheet went. This is just fucking devious."

"What the hell are you talking about?"

"A few months back, I thought one of my sheets disappeared from the hamper. It sounded crazy, so I convinced myself I was wrong."

"Why would anyone steal your dirty sheet and dress dolls in it?"

Bran cleared his throat. "It had my, umm, semen on it. Stuff like that comes in handy in magic."

Bran's embarrassment amused Denton no end. "Wow, if I knew witchcraft was so filthy, I would've gotten involved sooner. You'll have to tell me more." He gave Bran his cheesiest leer and topped it off with a wink.

"Stop goofing around. I'm serious."

Denton sighed. "Fine, fine. I don't get it, though. Did someone put a curse on you?" He looked at the dolls. "On us?" Denton couldn't imagine who or why anyone would wish them harm—aside from the usual assortment of assholes who loved to hate. But breaking and entering with voodoo dolls didn't sound like their style. Too subtle.

"Yep. My mother. But not a curse exactly."

"What? Why?"

"This is a love spell. She must have done it months ago."

Denton's mood brightened. "Really? I guess it worked." Not that he believed in love spells, but it was good to know nobody had tried to put bad juju on them.

"It's not the point. People shouldn't meddle in the lives of others. Especially their own children." Strangely, he glared at Murry while talking. The cat yawned and then scratched his ear with his hind paw.

Denton leaned closer and placed a kiss on Bran's spine. "I need to go. Should we put the mattress back first?"

"I'll need to buy a new one, but we might as well for now."

Denton took one last look at the strange symbol, which seemed to have been finger-painted in reddish-brown ink or something. A suspicious thought hit him. "Is this blood?"

"Probably. You don't wanna touch it," he added when Denton stretched his fingers toward the drawing.

"Why?"

"Some blood is more potent than others, and my mother isn't shy about these things."

"I don't understand."

"There's a reason only women can perform certain witchcraft."

At last, Denton added two and two together. "Oh. *Oh!*" He snatched his hand back. "You're a strange family."

"What gave you a clue?"

They put the bed back as it had been before, minus the dolls, which Bran shoved into a drawer. Denton leaned in for a kiss, putting his arms around Bran's waist. As they pulled apart, he gave Bran's buttocks a friendly squeeze. "Kilts—think about it."

***

A couple of minutes later, Denton sat in his own apartment, staring at the computer screen in sheer horror while talking to Joy on the phone. "This is hideous. Why did you make me look at this? What have I done to you?"

"It's work. We've been hired to redesign the site."

"Somebody has to, that's for sure. The whole thing is in Flash! With Mystery Meat navigation. And what the hell's up with the annoying music? How did this abomination even happen on the first place? Is this a legit business site or a joke?"

Joy let out an unladylike snort. "From what I gathered, the former head of marketing wanted the site to *pop*, and it just so happened that his second cousin was a hotshot Flash designer."

"It pops, all right. Where's this *former* marketing genius now?"

"Quit and went to the competition."

"Ouch. Talk about scorched earth."

"No kidding. The director, Mr. Barnaby, is keen on getting their website back to sane. Customers have been complaining. I need you to look it over, come up with a proposal for site structure, function, et cetera, that I can present tomorrow. I'm e-mailing you their list of requirements. I need the stuff from you by tomorrow morning."

"Not last minute at all," Denton grumbled.

"I'm buying you breakfast," Joy said in a honey-dipped voice.

"I want chocolate croissants. Plural."

"You got it."

***

Denton approached Alice's Tea Room from a different direction this time to avoid the unpleasant death trace of the guy who'd died there recently. According to Bran, he should be better at shielding them out now that he'd been practicing, but he didn't feel up to testing the theory right then. From this new direction, only a lone spirit stood in his path, but she didn't bother him. Steering around the hazy shape, Denton could tell it was a woman and even make out the paisley pattern of her dress. A blast of sweet perfume basted his senses as he walked past. These things were new. The more he trained, the more clearly he could see the spirits, and for the first time he experienced the occasional olfactory impressions too.

He spotted Joy coming from the opposite direction, bundled in a big coat, her nose almost as red as the scarf around her neck. They met at the door, then stepped out of the chilly November air and into the warm café together. They found a table under a painting of the March Hare.

Once Denton had his coffee and promised pastries in front of him, they got down to business. Joy showed him her design concepts for approval, although she didn't have to. Denton had no artistic talent of his own and trusted hers completely. Next he explained what he thought would be the most user-friendly site navigation and what new features they should add and explained their benefits. Joy nodded, asked a few questions, and took notes.

"I think this site will be our best one yet," she said.

"When do we start working?"

"Mr. Barnaby will have to get budget approval and stuff, but I don't think it'll take more than a week. Enjoy your freedom till then.

"You sure we'll get the job?"

"Positive. Mr. Barnaby loves our portfolio and is eager to erase all traces of his former marketing guy. I got the impression that, in his eyes, redesigning the site is the next best thing to hiring a hit man."

"All right. I'll start working on the wireframes."

"Good thinking." Joy gave him a squinty look and changed the direction of the conversation. "So you and Mr. Darcy are all hot and sticky now? I have a hard time imagining him in the throes of passion."

Denton managed to swallow his coffee and not laugh. "Hey, keep your filthy fantasies off my boyfriend!"

Joy smiled with deceptive sweetness. "Boyfriend, eh?"

"Yup." Denton didn't blush. It would've been unmanly.

She shook her head. "I still don't see it. The guy's just so…I dunno…stick-up-the-butt."

Denton rushed to Bran's defense. "He's really not once you get to know him. Bran's simply introverted and uneasy around strangers, that's all."

"If you say so, dog-breath." Joy didn't appear quite convinced. "Tell me about him. What does he do for a living?"

Denton raised the cup to his lips to buy himself time. The secrets he'd been keeping from Joy had been gnawing at him, so he was wary of piling on more. However, he couldn't betray Bran's confidence either. In the end, he decided to be frank about the obvious things. "He calls himself an herbalist and writes books about herbs, but he's also a witch."

Joy raised her left eyebrow a whole inch. "A witch?"

"Yes. A witch." Denton gave her a stubborn glare.

"Like Harry Potter and stuff?"

"No he doesn't use a wand, but he can make potions or spells. I think."

"Ah, Snape! But of course," Joy said, grinning.

Denton rolled his eyes and drank more coffee. Maybe this had been a mistake.

"Oh, don't get huffy. So Bran's a witch, fine. Wouldn't it be a wizard or warlock, by the way?"

"No, definitely not. I've been lectured on the subject. Males of their kind are called witches too. End of story."

"Good to know. I wouldn't want to be politically incorrect and offend the wrong coven. So, what, he spends his days brewing potions?"

"Actually, I haven't seen him do that, but his apartment smells like an herb garden, which it is, for the most part. Occasionally he does house cleansing for paid clients. I helped him a couple of times. It turns out I've got a knack for it. We banished a ghost from Sparks—you know, that restaurant you told me about?" He carefully didn't mention his own ghost-related talents.

Joy reached across the table and punched Denton in the shoulder. She had a sharp, bony fist. "No way!"

"Way," Denton replied, rubbing the sore spot.

"I heard rumors the place was cursed or haunted or something. What was it?"

"The ghost of an old gangster who got himself killed there back in the sixties."

"For real? That's so cool. You guys are like ghostbusters."

Joy seemed genuinely thrilled, and it made Denton happy, even if it meant merciless teasing for weeks or even months. He'd get that anyway. "So you don't think it's weird?"

"Oh, it totally is. But so are you. You can't even walk down the street in a straight line. But I love you anyway. Have to admit, you two whackadoodles make perfect sense together. But I still want to check Bran out for myself." The sudden grooves on her forehead spelled trouble. "I know what, Thanksgiving! Unless you're visiting your family."

Denton considered lying, but he just couldn't. "No, not this year."

"Excellent! We'll have dinner. I'll cook."

Trouble, indeed.

"Ugh. Do you have to?"

Denton had been a victim of Joy's cooking before and didn't wish to repeat the experience. Her bouts of culinary fervor were unpredictable and always disastrous. After admitting defeat, she'd put away the recipes, and a period of peace would follow. Till the next time. The enthusiastic gleam in her eyes was a bad sign.

She beamed at Denton with the smile of eternal optimists. "Nah, don't worry. It'll be good. I got new cookbooks."

"You said the same thing last time."

Joy dismissed his protest with a flick of her wrists. "Martha Stewart was a mistake. Too fussy. I bought three of Jamie Oliver's books. His recipes are simple, healthy, and he's totally cute."

Denton had no idea who that was, but it didn't matter. He admitted defeat. Nothing short of a natural disaster would stop Joy once she had her mind set. He could only hope Bran wouldn't say anything too blunt. Assuming he agreed to the dinner in the first place.

Joy gathered up the sheets of paper and shoved them into her bag. "Listen, I'd love to gab, but if I don't skedaddle, I'll be late for this meeting. I'll call you later and we'll talk, 'kay?"

They hugged, kissed, and parted ways, but Denton had barely taken three steps down the street before he heard Joy yelling his name. He spun around.

"Remember, don't cross the beams!" she shouted loud enough for the whole block to hear. Random strangers snapped their heads toward her and Denton. She ignored her unintended audience and dashed away.

An older guy and his terrier gave Denton strange looks.

"And she calls me a weirdo," he told them. He turned and moved on before either the man or the dog could reply.

***

Later that day, Denton let himself into Bran's apartment with his own key and found Bran at the kitchen table, surrounded by piles of cut herbs and Ziploc bags, stuffing the former into the latter.

Bran looked up, nodded, and kept talking into the phone stuck between his shoulder and ear. "Payable in advance. You get a full refund if the haunting doesn't stop. … Yes, you'd have to take my word for it. If you find the terms unacceptable—" His free shoulder slumped in resignation. "I see. … You will? … I don't know. I'll call you when it's done. Good-bye." Bran hung up.

"Another smudging?" Denton asked, pulling a chair out for himself. He made a mental note to get Bran a Bluetooth headset for Christmas.

"Yup. Real estate agent, having trouble selling a property—supposedly it's haunted. She'll messenger a check and the keys over."

"Wow. She must be in a hurry."

Bran shook his head. "I don't understand. The more outrageous the fees I charge, the more people want to hire me. It makes no sense."

"It's psychology. If you're expensive, people will think of your services as a rare treat they can have because they have money. It makes them feel special. Like caviar."

"Caviar?"

"Yeah, it's just fish eggs. Kinda gross, if you ask me. So how did she hear of you?"

Bran grimaced. "Sparks."

"Damn the man for driving business your way!"

"It's not funny," Bran said, but a smile played hide-and-seek on his lips.

"What's up with the baggies? Are you dealing?"

"One of my mother's old friends runs a small deli, and she can sell my extra herbs. I have too much and hate to throw them away. I don't take money from her, but she always forces some goods on me. Maybe we'll get caviar."

Bran made a face. "Great. Can I help?"

"You can put the labels on." Bran demonstrated how to place the printed label at the lip of the baggie and fold it over so the herb's name showed on one side.

Denton copied him but immediately messed it up.

"No, that's the wrong label," Bran chided him. "Can't you tell the difference between basil and oregano?"

"No," Denton admitted.

Bran let out a heavy sigh and arranged some baggies into one pile, others into another. "This is oregano, and that's basil."

They all still looked the same to Denton, so he just took Bran at his word.

They bagged, labeled, had lunch; then the courier arrived with a padded envelope, which contained a check, a key, and a sticky note with an address.

***

Irina's Deli turned out to be a hole-in-the-wall shop with shelves crammed full of boxes, jars, cans, and bottles of imported goods. Irina Bosko herself turned out to be a white-haired old lady presiding behind the cash register. A younger woman, who could've been her granddaughter, busied herself behind the counter.

After patting them on the cheeks and asking Bran about his mother, Irina let them go on the condition that they'd take several pairs of smoked sausages and a candy bar with them.

"Oh, this is so good," Denton said, chewing on a piece of chocolate, once they were back in the car and on their way again. "Sure you don't want some?"

Bran shook his head and kept his eye on the traffic.

"She seemed like a nice old lady."

"I've been coming to the store since I was two. I suspect she's spying on me for Mother." Bran smiled as he said it, but Denton got the impression he wasn't entirely joking. He also wondered if Bran brought him along to send a message to Mrs. Maurell. Weird family.

They drove on in silence till the car came to a halt on a quiet, residential street in Old Town. Their destination was one of the twelve condos in a red brick building, which, by its appearance, had been there long enough to accumulate history and a ghost or two. The trees on the street were bare now, but from spring to fall they must have provided a pleasant view.

Bran and Denton let themselves in and wandered around. The living room showed signs of recent remodeling. As the agent had informed Bran, the unit was unoccupied and unfurnished.

"Do you see anything?" Bran asked.

Denton shook his head.

The kitchen sparkled with granite countertops and brushed aluminum appliances.

Bran took the top sheet from the stack of real estate flyers on the counter. "Two bedrooms, one bath, a thousand square feet," he read out loud. "They are asking two-hundred grand, down from two seventy-five. That's a big drop, even in this market."

"The agent said they had lots of viewers but not a single offer."

"Because of the ghost?"

"She thinks so. She also said the place has an eerie vibe."

"Very scientific."

They found nothing of interest in either of the bedrooms but hit pay dirt in the bathroom. Denton sensed the "eerie vibe" from down the hallway—it felt like pure misery. No wonder no one wanted to live here. Bran, who must've felt it too, brushed his hand against his in a reassuring gesture.

At first Denton saw nothing inside the bathroom, aside from more gleaming white tiles and granite, but he distinctly heard water splashing and a clink of glass against a hard surface. And sobbing.

"Definitely haunted." He kneeled down, reached out, and touched the edge of the empty tub. That was when things got wonky. A curtain of steam rose out of nothing in front of his eyes. Denton rocked back on his heels and bumped into Bran's legs.

Wisps of haze arranged themselves into a shape of a man. Denton could make out the figure sitting in the spot he'd touched a minute ago.

Bran lowered himself to his knees and whispered into Denton's ear, "You see it too?" His words came out as barely more than puff of air brushing Denton's skin.

Denton nodded, not taking his eyes off the apparition. He took a deep breath and let the light fill him. Recalling how he'd banished spirits before, he raised his right hand with palm open and turned outward. To his surprise, the spirit mirrored his movements and their fingers touched. Sort of. There was no tactile sensation, but an overwhelming sense of anguish flowed into Denton. His common sense told him to break contact, but the desire to learn more wouldn't let him. He concentrated on the emotion, immersed himself in it, and realized the ghost was waiting. Who knew how long he'd been doing that very thing, and most certainly for someone who'd never come.

Denton felt genuinely sorry for this stranded spirit and wished he could help. But of course, the best he could do was to send it packing. He focused on the light again, pulling it into him and directing it outward. However, because of pity he felt for the spirit, he let it out in a gentle stream rather than the usual quick blast. Unexpectedly, the ghost didn't disappear but instead became more distinct.

Bran's breath caught. "Stop!" He yanked Denton's hand back. "What are you doing?"

"I don't know. I thought I was banishing it."

A semitransparent blond man in his twenties stared at them. His lips parted, and a perfectly normal human voice emerged from them. "Who are you?"

Chapter Two

Oh hell. Denton had plenty of experience with dead people, but none had ever initiated a conversation. Well, when in Rome…or whatever. There was only one thing to do.

He cleared his throat. "I'm Denton, and this is Bran. What's your name?"

"Will. What are you doing here? Are you Gene's friends?"

"Umm, yes, sure. We're here to see you, Will. Do you have a last name?"

Will froze. "Is that the doorbell?"

"No, I don't think—"

The ghost leapt up and bolted out of the room, with no concern for Denton and Bran being in the way. A nauseating chill passed through Denton. He saw Bran shudder. "Did you feel that?"

"Hell, yes."

They found Will standing in the middle of the living room, looking lost.

"Let me try this alone," Denton whispered to Bran, who nodded and stayed at the doorway.

Denton circled around Will to face him. He was the most well-defined ghost Denton had ever clapped eyes on. Denton could clearly make out his flared jeans and his retro-style yellow shirt with a wide collar. To top it off, through his partially see-through body Denton saw not the beige walls of their current surroundings but the loud patterns of old wallpaper.

Denton waved his hand. "Hey, Will. You okay?" As he seemed to have gotten the ghost's attention, he went on. "Who are you waiting for?"

"Gene. He should be here any moment."

"Gene who?"

"I should've gone to meet him, but he said not to bother."

Denton tried again. "Does Gene have a last name?"

Alas, Will was on his own track. "I always knew he'd come around. It's been three years, but he finally called. He said he was sorry, and he wanted to start over, do it right this time."

"Hey, Will, over here. What's your full name? What year is this?"

Will didn't even acknowledge him. Instead, he stared toward the entrance. "Is that the doorbell?"

Denton skipped to the side before Will could pass through him again. With inhuman speed, Will zapped to the door, but then stopped like a reverse vampire. Although, to the best of Denton's knowledge, the whole thing about vampires not being able to cross a threshold without invitation was hogwash.

Will drifted back to the middle of the room.

Denton chose a different approach. "Will, tell me about Gene. The two of you together."

This proved to be the right thing to say. Will turned, although it was hard to tell if his eyes looked at or through Denton. "We said such terrible things to each other last time. I called him a fake and a liar. He…he said things too. But I always know he couldn't deny what he was, what we were for each other." He darted to the window and lifted the blinds that weren't there. "He should be here by now. What could be keeping him?"

At a loss, Denton decided to try honesty. "You're dead and have been for a while. Whoever Gene is, I don't think he'll come. You'd be better off going yourself. I can help."

Will didn't seem to have heard a word. "Is that the doorbell?"

Denton sighed. He got ready to blast the ghost for good, but before he could, Will shot off toward the bathroom. Denton and Bran followed but found the room empty. They could hear water filling the tub, although it was still bone dry. Denton touched its edge like he'd done before, but nothing happened. Will didn't manifest again.

Denton turned to Bran, who kept glaring at the tub. "You saw him too, right?"

"Bright as day, and if I did, so would anyone else. This is not good."

"I know. What do we do now?"

"We go home and regroup."

Bran stayed far too quiet even for him during the whole trip. At home, they wordlessly parted to their own apartments. Denton tried to work on the website, but he couldn't concentrate. Finally, he gave up and went over to Bran's. He found Bran, nose buried in the tome they'd been using for his necromancer training.

"Found anything useful?" he asked.

"Not really. There's a lot here about summoning a spirit, but you didn't exactly. You made it more visible." Irritation abraded Bran's words. "What the hell were you thinking?"

"I wasn't. I felt sorry for the guy. You could feel his misery too, couldn't you?"

Bran slammed the book closed. "That's not the point. We were there for a purpose—get rid of a spirit, not bring it more into this realm."

"Well, sorry. Shit happens."

Bran clenched his jaws and said nothing. Denton didn't understand his mood. "Okay, so I improvised. If everything else fails, they make the place into a sideshow. It would rake in the money."

The joke didn't go over well at all. "We go back tomorrow and smudge the condo the old-fashioned way. I don't want you to be doing any improvising," Bran said in an and-that's-final voice and walked out of the room.

"Don't you even wonder who Gene was?" Denton shouted after him.

"No."

Denton threw himself onto the sofa. He opened the book but couldn't read a single word, and the convoluted illustrations only made him more frustrated. A firm nudge in his ribs alerted him of Murry's presence. The cat rubbed his face against Denton's abs and kneaded Denton's thighs with his front paws.

"Watch those nails," Denton warned him.

Murry purred louder than a small airplane engine, and it resonated through his whole body, into Denton's fingers digging into his fur. He was definitely a bit plump, but it felt good to the touch. After about ten minutes of furry love-fest, Denton felt much better.

"I'll go check on Mr. Grumpy," he said, transferring Murry from his lap to the cushions. Murry lifted a leg to give his privates a bath.

Denton found Bran in the kitchen working on dinner. He was still annoyed, Denton could tell. He didn't bang pots and pans, like ordinary people would. No, his movements were measured and precise. Everything under control.

Denton watched the taut lines of his back before speaking up. "What's cooking?"

"Herbed chicken breast with rice and salad," Bran replied without turning from the stove.

He enjoyed cooking and was good at it too. Unsurprisingly, he excelled at the use of fresh herbs. There was a pile of them now on the counter, waiting to be chopped.

"Need help?" Denton asked.

"I'm fine."

Crabby pants. Denton preferred dealing with trouble head-on. "You know, you can just shout at me, if it makes you feel any better."

That got Bran's attention. He turned. "Shout?"

Denton shrugged. "Yeah, sure. We scream at each other for a couple of minutes, then go back to normal. I'm still not clear what got you so worked up, but you have to let the pressure out somehow. Bottling it up won't do you much good. One day you'll blow like Mount St. Helens."

Denton must've hit a nerve, because Bran cast his eyes down. "I suppose you have a point. But I don't want to scream at you."

"All right. What if I give you a blowjob, then? Since we're on the subject of blowing already."

"What?" Bran snapped his eyes up.

Denton waggled his studded brow suggestively. Causing bewilderment was the first part of his plan to diffuse Bran's mood. "Orgasm are proven to relieve stress. So, how about it? I blow you, we eat, and then you blow me?" It was a good plan. He thought so, at any rate.

At long last, the storm clouds lifted from Bran's face. "Okay."

Denton stepped right up and reached for Bran's belt.

"Wait! The rice," Bran protested.

"The rice will be fine."

***

The rice got mushy, but they happily ate it anyway. After Bran returned the favor, they fell asleep in his bed. Denton hardly spent any time in his own these nights, and that was fine with him. He preferred drifting off next to a warm body and waking up huddled behind his lover, Bran's tail resting between his thighs. On this fine morning, said appendage gave Denton all kinds of naughty ideas, but his bladder had others. He slipped out from under the covers and made a beeline for the bathroom.

On his way back to bed, he noticed something seriously amiss in the living room. The dark-haired woman sitting in one of the chairs definitely hadn't been there the night before. As she watched him with unconcealed interest, Denton couldn't tell if her presence or his own nakedness perturbed him more. Possibly the combination of the two. He retreated into the bedroom and shook Bran by the shoulders. He got a sleepy grumble in response.

Denton shook him again. "Wake up. There's a strange woman in your living room."

Bran cracked his eyes open. "What does she look like?" he asked in a voice thick with sleep and wariness but not shock.

Denton recalled her image. "Lots of dark hair. Attractive but not too young." From that brief look, Denton guessed her age at late thirties, maybe well-preserved forties. "She's wearing a green dress."

Bran rubbed his eyes and groaned. "Oh, great." He rolled out of bed and threw on his jeans and a clean shirt.

Denton followed suit. He half expected the woman to be gone, but when they got to the living room door, she still sat there, exactly as before.

"Where?" Bran asked.

"Right there, in the chair. Can't you see her?"

Bran let out a sigh. "Mother, you can stop it now. He can see you. I told you he would."

She did a weird flickering thing and hopped up. "You did, honey, but I had to test it for myself." She strolled up and turned her eyes on Denton. They were almost as dark as Bran's. "Denton, right? Bran told me about you. Not a lot, mind you. I have to pull the words out of him with pliers sometimes."

"You don't look old enough to be Bran's mom." The words tumbled out of his mouth.

Her face broke out in a wide smile, and she patted his cheeks. "You're sweet. Bran told me you were."

"I said he had a sweet tooth," Bran interjected.

"Pish-posh. You look like a nice young man, Denton, even with those things in your face. It's fashionable among youth these days, I know. Oh well, it'll pass. It's nice to meet you at last."

"It's nice to meet you too, Mrs. Maurell."

"It's Ms. I never married. But call me Layla."

"What was the flickering thing you did?" Denton recalled Bran doing it once, back around the time they'd first met.

"Invisibility spell, but it didn't fool you. I've heard this about necromancers, but I've only met one once before, long time ago when I was a young girl. He was quite a character."

"Mother, you could've let me know me you were coming to visit," Bran said.

"I could've, but it would've ruined the surprise." She circled her arms around Bran and planted a kiss on his cheek. "The food on the plane was ghastly. Would you mind whipping up one of those herb omelets you do so well?" she asked, releasing him. "Denton and I will chat out on the balcony, right, Denton?"

"Umm, okay."

"You better put on shoes and a sweater, hon. You're awful skinny. Do you eat right?"

"It's my metabolism."

Denton put on some more clothing to insulate himself, and then he and Layla settled into a couple of patio chairs. Over to their left, the blasted pigeons were congregating on Denton's fire escape, as usual.

Layla took in the gray skies. "So gloomy. In California, you get used to the constant sunshine. After a while, you take it for granted."

"Do you come back often?"

She shook her head. "I hate flying. It's so depressing—a bunch of irritable strangers stuffed together like sardines in a can. And to think it used to be glamorous. I'm trying to convince Bran to visit me instead. I'm only here because one of my old clients needs my help. He's in the middle of arranging a business merger, but something's fishy."

Apropos, fishy. "We found the spell under the bed." Denton expected a guilty reaction but was disappointed.

"You did? When?"

"A few days ago."

"Very good. You don't need it anymore. It was one tricky piece of witchcraft, I can tell you. I had to ask Bran's father to help. Mal can be such a hard case—I'm afraid Bran inherited his stubbornness—but he understood the necessity once I properly explained it to him."

"Are you saying Bran and I like each other only because you cast some spell?" Denton heard the aggravated rasp in his own voice, but he couldn't help it.

Layla laughed, and startled pigeons threw themselves into the air. "Not at all, honey. I don't do those sort of love charms, and I tell my clients too—those might work for a while, but if you're not a good match, all the magic in the world won't keep you together. They don't much like hearing it, but tough."

"Okay, I'm lost. What *did* you cast?"

"Oh, a little something I've learned from my grandmother—part love spell, part summoning. Its purpose is to attract a person's perfect mate."

"No offense, Ms. Maurell, but—"

"Layla."

As she smiled, Denton saw the spider webs of age around her eyes, but she still looked far too young. She had to be in her fifties at least. Must be magic.

"Ehrm…Layla, I have a hard time believing you can simply conjure up somebody's soul mate."

She gave her a pitying look. "You ever wonder how convenient it was for you and Bran to meet, considering your talents and peculiarities that you can't share with other people?"

"It only means we're a good professional match."

"Well, there's more to it, isn't it? I saw you earlier in each other's arms. Sleeping bodies don't lie."

Denton flushed hot from his chest to the tips of his ears. Not only had Bran's mother had seen him naked, but she'd seen them in bed together. Suddenly he understood Bran's exasperation.

Unperturbed by Denton's embarrassment, she chattered on. "I don't believe there's only one soul mate for each of us, but for boys like you and Bran who are more unique, it can be hard to find a compatible partner. And, of course, with Bran's refusal to even try, it was never going to happen. I had to do something. I couldn't let him spend his whole life alone just because of one bad experience."

Denton's curiosity perked up. "Bad experience?"

Layla leaned closer and lowered her voice. "He got involved with an older man when he was very young and impressionable. I could've told him a thirty-year-old had no business sniffing around a sixteen-year-old, but teenage boys don't talk to their mothers. Things got ugly when this man humiliated Bran in public."

"I killed him," Bran said from the doorway, making them both jump a little. They turned to see him there, hands on hips. "And whatever faults Peter had, he didn't deserve that."

Layla recovered faster. "Honey, you're exaggerating. You didn't kill him."

"I turned him into a frog."

Denton's jaw dropped. "You did what?"

A shadow of pain or guilt, or possibly both, flickered across Bran's face. "I tried to catch him, but he hopped away, straight into the pond."

Layla clearly had no sympathy for this Peter person. "He deserved it, if you ask me. What kind of a man calls a young boy a freak, especially in front of strangers? At any rate, it's not the same as killing him."

"He's probably been eaten by an animal or run over by a car by now."

"Those count as natural causes for a frog. It all happened fourteen years ago. Peter probably lived a far more fulfilling, not to mention useful life as an amphibian. The Lily Pond at Lincoln Park is the perfect place for it."

"You don't know that for sure."

Her voice grew sharper. "And you don't know otherwise. You were going to live your entire life like a hermit because of one little mishap. It's not healthy. And neither is suppressing your talents."

Bran's jaw set stubbornly. "Breakfast is getting cold."

He marched inside, and they followed him. The tranquility of clattering china and silverware settled over them for a few minutes. Denton shoveled heaps of the omelet into his mouth while also chewing on the fresh information. It wasn't every day you found out your lover could…what was the word they used in the Harry Potter books? Oh yeah, *transfigure* another person. Pretty cool.

Curiosity got the best of him. "How did you do it?"

Bran kept his eye on his plate and remained silent, so Layla filled in the void. "Spontaneous spell throwing is not uncommon for a young witch. When I was thirteen, I made it snow inside our apartment once. You should've seen my mother's face! Puberty is a difficult phase, but once your hormones and talents balance out, these things don't happen anymore. It's no reason to completely suppress your natural abilities." She put a strong emphasis on her words.

They weren't lost on Bran. "Mother, you've always overestimated my so-called abilities. They are as random and pointless as your moments of clairvoyance. I mean, honestly, what use was it to know Mrs. Samadis would cook lamb on a certain night? They cooked lamb at least once a week."

She let out a sigh. "Mrs. Samadis was very hospitable and an excellent cook. She also liked her and her husband's fortune being read. Bran, honey, you have the gift, like it or not. It's flowing out of your every pore. Do you think that jungle there is an accident?" She gestured toward the windows and the profusion of greenery surrounding them. "The best gardener can't grow them so healthy and abundant."

"Maybe I should get a job at the botanical garden."

Her fork clattered to the plate. "You're as stubborn as a mule." She turned to Denton. "How about you? Are you mastering your skill yet?"

"Umm… I made a ghost more corporeal instead of banishing it."

Her eyes lit up. "Really? How interesting. Visible to the naked eye?"

"Bran could see it. And we had a conversation. Sort of. Will's a bit of a broken record, responds to some questions but then goes off on his own tangent, and it's like talking to a wall. One thing's certain, he's fixated on someone called Gene—he's waiting for the guy."

She nodded. "That makes sense. Even more visible, it's a spirit shadow, not a complete person. Obsession tends to stick around the most. What do you plan to do about it?"

"I'll smudge it," Bran said.

"I doubt you can. Sounds too strong for it now."

Bran sighed. "Well, then Denton can expel it. He's done it a few times before."

She hummed in a tone expressing doubt.

"What's wrong with *that* plan?" Bran asked.

"I'm not convinced it'll work either, with Denton not fully in charge of his skills. And if you're not careful, you might make the situation worse."

Bran threw up his hands. "What are we supposed to do, then?"

"Well, spirits stick around for all sorts of reasons. Sometimes because they have unfinished business. If you help them find closure, they'll leave on their own. At least that's what my grandmother told me."

Bran's gloomy expression showed he didn't much like hearing her advice.

Layla pushed her chair back. "I'm sorry, Denton, for dragging you into our family drama. Please, be patient with my son. He means well."

Denton grinned back at her. "You got it, Layla."

"Good. I have to go. Behave yourselves, kids, and Bran, I want to spend some time with both of you before flying back to LA."

"Yes, Mother."

Chapter Three

Denton took the initiative to wash the dishes. He didn't mind, and he much preferred it to cooking. Fair division of labor, he figured. Bran helped with the drying.

During this domestic tranquility, Denton had a chance to think about their spirit problem. "We should go back and try to question Will again," he suggested.

"No way. Not till we find out more about him."

Typical Bran, Denton thought. "Do you ever just do something without making plans first? You know, go with the flow?"

"No," Bran replied brusquely.

"I didn't think so. Okay, Captain, what do we do next?"

Bran pinched his nose. "David from the Historical Society won't be any help here. Finding out who lived at that address forty years ago will be a challenge. According to the real estate agent, it was an apartment building till ninety-six, then converted to condos. So Will was a renter. We can start with finding the original owner on the slight chance they still have records."

"Ugh." Denton hadn't realized ghost hunting had so many complications.

They finished the dishes, and Bran wandered back into the living room with a look of consternation on his face and digging his fingers into his trapezius. Denton recognized the signs. "Sit. I'll give you a back rub."

"I'm fine."

"No, you're not," Denton said in his take-no-shit voice.

Bran gave in and settled sideways on the couch. Denton sat behind him and began to knead Bran's neck and shoulders. "You're all knotted up."

"Having a long conversation with Mother does it to me every time."

"I like her. She's certainly…spirited."

"That's one way of putting it."

Murry trotted into the room and hopped onto the chair across from them. Giving them a bored look, he curled up for a nap.

Denton's mother would've loved Murry, but then she loved all animals. No wonder when she remarried, it was to a veterinarian.

"My mom fusses all the time and keeps asking if I've met someone nice yet. Oh, that reminds me—do you think Layla might stay till Thanksgiving? It's only a couple of weeks away," Denton said.

Bran grew even more rigid under his fingers. "Don't even mention it to her!"

"What, Thanksgiving?"

"Yes! She only celebrates pagan holidays. Beltane, summer solstice, that sort of stuff. As a child, it took me a while to realize that half-naked people dancing around bonfires was not how most people celebrated holidays."

The image made Denton chuckle.

"Don't laugh," Bran grumbled. "If you bring up Thanksgiving or any other conventional holiday in front of her, you'll get an hour lecture."

"All right, I won't. Now try to relax." Denton went on smoothing the gnarls and lumps out of Bran's muscles. He knew he had a knack for it.

Bran thought so too. "Mmm…that's good. A little to the left. Yeah. Harder. You have magic fingers."

"I've been told that before. And not only in connection with back rubs."

Bran leaned into his touch without comment. Denton bit his lips to keep himself from saying more and have Bran tense up again. There was an intimate subject he didn't know how to approach. Denton wasn't strictly a bottom. Men tended to assume so simply because of his physique, but in the past, he had disabused many of them of that notion, to mutual satisfaction. He itched to do the same to Bran, but Bran… Well, he was a hard nut to crack. It was unlikely Bran had ever bottomed for anyone. Denton had to proceed with caution and wait for the right moment.

And that reminded him of a question he had. "Was it because of your tail that guy…Peter, called you a freak?"

Bran nodded. "Easy guess, right?"

"Were you afraid it would happen again? That you'd turn someone into something else?"

Bran pulled away and leaned back on the sofa. "When it happened, I was hurt and angry. More than angry, enraged. I didn't mean to do anything, but all the emotions burst out of me and BAM!" He turned his palms up, fingers stretched wide apart, in the imitation of an explosion. Then he curled them up again and put his hands in his lap. He looked Denton squarely in the eye. "Yes, I was afraid. Up till then, I had no idea of the destructive potential of the thing inside me. I knew I had to get my emotions under wraps and avoid any situation where something similar could happen again."

"That explains a few things. Surely by now you could control it."

"That's easy for you and Mother to say. Sometimes I'm scared to death I might hurt you."

The sincerity of the admission hit Denton in the chest. "You wouldn't."

"I'm not sure."

"I am." Denton didn't know what made him so certain, but the conviction came from his gut. You couldn't argue with instincts.

Bran's expression softened. "That's because you're a nut."

"Yeah. What's your point?"

"Haven't you ever wished you were normal like everyone else?"

"Yes, sure. But I'm not, and neither are you. It's much better to be weirdos together than alone. Your mom's right."

Bran turned his gaze at the ceiling and said nothing.

Denton scuttled closer and threw his legs across Bran's thighs. "Hey, do you think our ghost and that Gene guy he's waiting for were lovers?"

"I got that impression. Although, Will's babble was a bit vague." The weight of his hands felt good on Denton's knees.

"That could've been because of the times. Did you get a good look at his clothes? So seventies."

Bran chuckled. "Those flared pants, and that shirt! Very *Saturday Night Fever.*"

"The hair too. Reminded me of Bo Duke from *The Dukes of Hazzard.* I loved that show as a kid. Sexy cars, sexy guys—what's not to like, right?"

"Right."

Denton laced his fingers with Bran's. "I wonder if Gene looks like Luke at all. Looked." Verb tenses got complicated when talking about the partially departed—which Gene might or might not be. He could even be alive and well, even if elderly.

Denton tried to picture Gene, but instead, Will's miserable expression kept floating into his mind. The desperation he'd felt when first touching the ghost rose up from his memory, almost as if it was his own. A terrible certainty took over—Gene would never come, and Will knew it. Yet Will waited anyway. Denton squeezed Bran's hand, hoping to use Bran's solidity to chase away the unpleasant feelings, but right then Bran made a strange face—eyes shut, features contorted into a grimace.

"Are you all right?" Denton asked in sudden alarm.

Bran lifted a hand in a halting gesture. For several heart-pounding seconds, they stayed there, frozen, while panicky thoughts zapped through Denton's brain, too fast to be recognizable. From the corner of his eye, he saw Murry sit up in his chair and stare.

Then Bran's features smoothed out, and he let out a long breath. "Five-five-three," he said, opening his eyes.

"What the hell was that?" Denton demanded to know. "You scared the hell out of me."

"Sorry. I had an extrasensory episode."

Denton's heartbeat gradually returned to normal. "You mean a vision?"

"Yeah."

"Oh? Do you think it has to do with Gene?"

"Well, I was thinking of him, trying to picture him, so maybe. It's how I had these...visions in the past."

"What did you see?"

"Nothing more than jumbled images of a wreckage—twisted metal, fire, that sort of stuff."

"What about five-five-three?"

"I don't know. It popped into my head. See, this is what I tried to explain to my mother—completely useless."

"I dunno…" Denton had another idea—he was unstoppable today. "Let's Google it!"

"What, you're just gonna type *wreckage* and *553* in a search engine?"

"Why not?"

Without waiting for a response, Denton jumped up, scuttled into Bran's study, and plopped in front of the computer. He indeed typed *553* and *wreckage* into the search field and hit return. The top result turned out to be an article about a Cessna crashing near Las Vegas. The year — 2003—was all wrong. He scrolled past a couple of links and clicked on a promising one. A quick scan of the page revealed it to be a Watergate-related conspiracy theory, but by the third paragraph, he knew he was on the right track.

"Bingo!" he announced.

"What is it?" Bran asked.

"United Air Flight 553 crashed near Chicago on its way to land at Midway. And the date is, guess what? 1972!" He turned and triumphantly beamed at Bran. "This must be it!"

"Maybe."

"You're a real wet blanket, you know."

"I'm merely circumspect. However, this is something David should be able to find information about. Maybe even a passenger list. I'll call him."

Bran's pussyfooting couldn't dampen Denton's self-satisfaction. "What did people do before the Internet?" he wondered out loud.

"Go to the library, talk to people, ask questions?" Bran said on his way out the door, jabbing at the keypad of his phone.

"Sounds tedious."

"Right."

Denton kept reading the article. It proved interesting. Among the victims were a congressman, a CBS reporter, and the wife of one of the Watergate conspirators. According to the conspiracists, secret agents swarmed the crash site within minutes. It seemed a bit far-fetched to Denton, and he moved on to check his e-mail. He found a few offers for dog food coupons and male-enhancement products, all of which he swiftly redirected into the spam folder. He opened a message from Joy, but it contained only a selection of ghost-themed lolcats and an assurance about getting the contract for the job soon. Denton Googled a lolcat fairy and attached it to his reply, saying she better be right, because he needed the money. The holidays were coming, and he had gifts to buy.

He found Bran tending to his plants—watering, pruning, and stroking their leaves. He was practically petting them. The herbs were bursting with life, so possibly Layla had been right. Denton decided to keep his mouth shut about it.

"What's the word?" he asked instead.

"David will call back tonight," Bran said, turning around. Maybe it was a trick of the light, but Denton could've sworn some of the plants stretched their tiny stems toward him.

"We could try to find out more about Will online till then."

Bran shook his head. "You can often find out a lot if you have a name, but the results of address searches get unreliable beyond a couple of decades. Plus the sites doing it want money.."

"You've done this before."

"Five hours of my life I'll never get back."

"Maybe you should hire a professional. Gabe's a private detective, you know."

"He is?"

"Well, he got his license because he has friends in dubious places, but he's been taking classes."

"Maybe later. Let's wait to see what David comes up with first."

"Okay, so what do we do till then?"

"Shower. Then it's time you learn how to summon a spirit."

"You think that's a good idea?"

"Knowing you, you'll probably do it by accident. It'll be much safer for everyone involved if you know the proper procedure."

***

The session started with Bran giving a lecture about summoning in general. Denton was surprised to learn about the variety of rituals and all the different props they used.

"I don't get it," he said. "What's all the fuss about? You summoned Esther Bernal's spirit easily enough, and there were no bronze daggers or wands in sight."

"What I performed was a basic ritual. Even then, the presence of Ashley and especially you in the circle boosted the spell's power. Most of all, I didn't conjure the spirit—she was already there. I merely made it move a few feet. You'll need something much stronger to reach Gene."

Bran went on in excruciating detail about the difference between summoning spirits and demons. "You don't want to accidentally end up with the wrong one. Spirits are only shadows of the once-living. Demons, on the other hand, are creatures with wills and minds of their own, and they are hard to control."

"Have you ever tried?"

Bran cleared his throat. "I can make my father appear, but it's because we share blood."

Denton's interest perked up. Bran's family was an endless source of fascination for him. "Interdimensional phone call. Awesome."

"Right." Bran flipped the pages of the book.

A funny idea leapt into Denton's head. "Could I summon you? I mean, if I learned how. You being part demon and all."

Bran gaped at him dumbstruck for several seconds. "I don't know," he said at last.

Denton's brain started to spin with the speed of a hamster wheel. "It could be wicked! I could transport you across town." The wheel wobbled. "Wait, maybe only your demon part would respond. Uh-oh, you could end up like one of those horrible transporter accidents on *Star Trek*. What if only your tail showed up?" Obviously, his hamster was on crack.

Bran stared at him in disbelief. "You're mad."

"Me? Never. Merely practical." Denton managed to keep a straight face for two whole seconds.

They took a break, during which Bran muttered under his breath about certain people who never took anything seriously. In response, Denton had a strategic conversation with Murry about how certain other people needed to learn to relax and just go with the flow every once in a while. The cat sprawled out on the carpet, eyes closed. He could've been asleep but for the twitching of the tip of his tail.

Denton spent the rest of the day memorizing incantations, the shapes and proper placements of symbols and runes and the words to recite when drawing them, plus the proper placement of specific objects when performing one ritual or the other. He took notes on a yellow legal pad, the pages of which were all crumpled and smudged by the time the sun went down. He doubted he'd ever be able to summon as much as a dead mouse.

The ringing of Bran's phone came as a welcome interruption. Especially since it was David calling. Denton kept his eyes on Bran's brows for clues.

"No Gene?… (downward slope—not good) Oh. Of course… (up-twitch—better) … He could be. Do you have surviving relatives? … Just a second." Bran made the handwriting sign in the air, and Denton quickly handed him the yellow pad and the pen.

Bran flipped to a clean page. "Okay, go." He began to write. "Right… Yes, thank you… Tell Amy hi… Okay. Talk to you later." Bran leaned back in his seat. Brushing his knuckles over his lips, he sank into contemplative silence.

Denton suppressed his urge to throttle him. "Are you planning to share?"

Bran blinked a few times and focused on Denton. "Oh. Sorry. The crash got a lot of media attention at the time, so David had no trouble digging up information. He found nobody with the name Gene among the victims, but one of the passengers who died was listed as Eugene Kent."

Denton thought it over. If his parents had named him Eugene, he'd prefer to be called Gene too. "Okay, he could be our guy. What do we do now?"

"The records listed Rosemary Dankworth, née Rosemary Kent, as the closest living relative. Eugene's sister."

"Oh. Well, at least it's not a common name. I bet we can find it on the Intraweb."

"Make it so, Number One." Bran lifted his hand and pointed in the direction of the study in an exact Captain Picard gesture.

This sudden outburst of frivolity took Denton completely by surprise. He stared mutely as Bran's solemn expression developed a smug undertone. He liked it.

Denton pulled himself up straight. "Aye, aye, Captain!" he said and bounded off toward the computer.

Locating Rosemary Dankworth took no time at all. The Pennsylvania phone number held promise—UA 553 had taken off from Washington DC. They agreed Denton should make the call, being the more sociable one.

The phone rang three times before a spry female voice answered, "Dankworth."

Denton's heart sank—she sounded far too young, twenties at most. "Can I talk to Mrs. Rosemary Dankworth, please," he asked.

"That's my grandma. Hang on."

While they waited, Denton grabbed a pen and the notepad from the desk.

"Hello. Who's this?" the woman asked at the other end of the line.

"Hi, Mrs. Dankworth. My name's Denton Mills, and I'm a writer from Chicago, doing research on the crash of Flight 553. Your brother Eugene Kent was on board, correct?"

He could hear only her breathing and the muffled sounds of television in the background for many seconds.

"Hello?" Denton said louder.

"Sorry, Mr…what did you say your name was…Mills?"

"Yes, but Denton will do, ma'am."

"Call me Rose, Denton."

"Rose, would you mind answering a few questions?"

She sighed. "Nobody has asked me about my Gene in decades, so it's a bit of a shock, you see. Why would you want to write about that old business now? It happened such a long time ago, nobody even remembers or cares anymore."

Scrambling for a reply, Denton remembered the date of the crash. "The fortieth anniversary is coming up in a couple of years. After 911, there's renewed interest because of the suspicious circumstances surrounding the accident."

"Oh, so you're one of those conspiracy theorists, then?"

Denton caught the bitterness in her tone and quickly backpedalled. "No, ma'am. My main interest is the human angle—you know, the regular people whose lives were cut short or altered forever by this tragedy. That's why I called you."

"I see. So how can I help you?" She sounded more cordial.

Denton didn't want to raise suspicion by starting with questions about her brother's connection to Will. Who knew what kind of history hid there? "Well, for a start, could you give me some background on your brother?"

135

The floodgates opened. She prattled on about Gene as a baby—three years younger than her—about them growing up, the scrapes he'd gotten into, the job Gene had at a local bank, and the bright future he should've had. "We were close—Gene was my little brother, and I felt responsible for him. It was hard on me when he died. I thought of him every day for years. Once my parents passed away, I had nobody left to talk to about him. My kids and grandkids never met Gene." Melancholy suffused her words. "I still dream of him sometimes. It's always the same—I'm at the airport waiting for him."

"May I ask why he was flying to Chicago?"

"To see Will."

"Will?" Denton hoped his voice didn't give away his excitement.

"Willard Hayes. They were best friends growing up. Inseparable. Then something happened between them. I don't know what, Gene wouldn't say. Will moved up to Chicago, went to work for one of the newspapers there. Not the Tribune, the other one. He'd always wanted to be a journalist. I wondered back then if Will's ambition was behind their fallout. It didn't make much sense, but you know how men are. In the end, they must've mended fences. I never heard from Will again, though. I found his address in Gene's things and sent an invitation for the memorial service, but he didn't come."

"Do you remember the address?"

"No, sorry, dear, not after all this time."

Bran grabbed the pad and pen and made a rushed scribble, which he held up. PHOTOGRAPH! it said.

Denton nodded to Bran and kept talking into the phone. "No problem. I didn't think you would. Can I trouble you for one more thing? Do you have a photograph of Gene I could have a copy of?"

"Sure, I can do that. You got me in the mood for looking through the old album. I'll have my granddaughter scan one of them and e-mail it to you. Is that all right? My grandkids send me pictures all the time."

"That would be great, thank you."

Denton waited for her to find pen and paper, then gave her his e-mail address. He thanked her again and said good-bye.

He turned to Bran. "Willard Hayes was Gene's best friend. He's a perfect candidate to be our Will, even without address confirmation."

"I'll go down to the Cook County Clerk's Bureau tomorrow and ask for the death record."

"And they'll just hand it to you?"

"People researching their ancestors go there all the time. The clerks know me there already as a genealogist."

"I see. Then what?"

"I have a plan. For now, we need to see if you've learned anything today," he said on his way out of the room.

Soon he was pushing the living room furniture to the walls and spreading a painter's drop cloth out on the floor. These preparations filled Denton with apprehension. Murry, on the other hand, surveyed the proceedings with keen interest from his usual post on the back of the sofa.

Bran left the room again and returned with a box of assorted items, including several candles, a rusty key, and chalk.

"Right. It's time you summon a spirit for real," he said.

"Who?" Denton wondered if there were easy-to-conjure practice spirits available for inexperienced necromancers.

"Peter."

Not the answer Denton expected. "Why on earth would you want me to do that?"

"Because I want to tell him I'm sorry."

The words fell between them, flat and cold, but Denton knew by now that Bran's impassive surface hid complicated emotions. Denton couldn't pin down exactly what bugged him most about the request. Jealousy? Or unease over Bran picking at an old scab? He thought of refusing but decided against it. Who knew, maybe it was closure Bran needed.

"Okay. What do I do?" he asked.

Bran told him which ritual to do—one of the simpler ones, thank God.

"This one requires a personal object," Denton said, consulting his notes.

Bran handed him a Polaroid photo of a man as unremarkable as a potted plant—not one of Bran's, but something you'd see in a bank lobby.

"Peter Lattimer," Bran explained.

Denton pointed at the pad. "This says you need something belonging to the deceased."

"Traditionally, you'd use a lock of hair or a piece of clothing, but for some reason, photographs work just the same."

"So it's true—they steal a part of your soul, after all," Denton quipped.

Bran shrugged. "Maybe they work because they also hold a trace of the living person? I don't know."

Denton went through his notes one more time, then stood at the edge of the drop cloth and laid down the necessary tools on the floor next to him. "Okay, I'm ready."

Bran turned off the lights and stood aside.

"Are you gonna help?" Denton asked.

"No. You should do this alone."

Denton waited for his eyes to get used to the semidarkness. The light of the moon and the city spilling through the windows gave just enough illumination to see what he was doing. The powdered sugar circle he drew around the photo turned out more of an oval, but it would have to do. He repeated the requisite chants as he put the candles at their places and lit them. At first he felt a little silly, but as he went on, the rhythm of the incantation got him into a groove. He picked up the chalk and drew the runes around the circle without having to check his cheat sheet.

He felt the warmth of light filling him as he stood at the edge of the drop cloth. He picked up the wand, which was more of a gnarly stick. Tracing the summoning symbol in the air, he loudly demanded the spirit of Peter Lattimer to appear. He had to repeat himself several times before the ring and the symbols around it began to give out a dim glow. And then…nothing happened. He redoubled his efforts and concentrated his thoughts on the man in the picture.

A gust of wind came out of nowhere. It made the candle light flare up for a moment, then die out completely and blew the summoning circle apart.

A loud "Meooowrr!" broke the dead silence.

Denton squinted as lamplight flooded the room. "What the fuck just happened?" he asked, glaring at Bran.

Bran came forward, picked up the Polaroid from the floor, and wiped it on his shirt. "The ritual failed. Damn. Look at the mess."

He was right—powdered sugar was everywhere.

They cleaned up and put everything back in its place. Murry played his part by supervising and being underfoot.

"Maybe Peter's not dead." Denton offered his opinion as they shifted the coffee table back to its usual spot.

"Not possible."

"Well, then, I suck at summoning."

"Even less likely." Bran threw himself into a chair. He drummed his fingers on the armrest while his whole face turned into a knot of anxiety.

Denton cast around for any reasonable explanation. "Okay, when you cursed him, Peter must have turned into a frog in more than just body. Or he wouldn't have hopped off into the water, right?"

Bran stopped drumming while he considered the question. "I suppose so. Not my area of expertise."

Encouraged by this admission, Denton went on. "You've told me that there are different rituals for summoning ghosts and demons. Wouldn't be logical that you need something else for animal spirits too?"

"That's possible. I haven't come across anything about animal spirits before," Bran said, scratching his chin.

"You just said it's not your field of expertise."

"Right. I'll have to do some research."

Denton was glad to see the prospect of a rational approach brighten Bran's mood. For a half demon, he was very methodical.

Murry hopped into Bran's lap, and then climbed on the chair's back and sprawled out in a pose that made him appear like a shawl around Bran's neck. His hind legs hung over one shoulder; his head peeked over the other. Bran in all black and with the cat behind him struck a picture-book image of a witch.

However, Denton was worn out by the whole occult business. "Can we have dinner? I'm starving."

Bran checked his watch. "Good idea. You'll need your strength."

Oh no. Denton didn't like the sound of that at all. No siree. "For what?"

"We'll have to go to the cemetery to collect graveyard dust. It's an exceptionally potent ingredient for conjuring."

Denton gaped at him. "You're not serious."

"I am."

Denton could tell Bran was indeed dead serious. "Isn't that illegal?"

"A little."

Murry lifted his head and fixed his gaze on Denton. His eyes, round as traffic lights, seemed to say: *GO. Nothing's wrong with a little trespassing. The dead don't mind.*

Denton gave in. "I... Okay, let's just go now and get it over with."

"Can't. It has to be done at midnight."

Denton slapped his forehead in exasperation. "You're as impossible as your cat."

"Ah, that. Murry's not my cat."

"What the hell do you mean? Whose cat is he?" Midnight loitering in cemeteries he could see, but catnapping?

"No. I mean he's my familiar. You know, demonic companion, etcetera? A gift from my father for my seventeenth birthday."

"Oh." Well, sure, it made sense. "He's still a cat, though," Denton pointed out.

"Most of the time."

"What do you mean *most of the time*?" Denton felt a headache coming on.

"On occasion, he can be a raven, Right, Murmur?"

Murry twitched his tail. "*Meowrr.*"

Chapter Four

"I'm surprised you asked Layla to come too," Denton said as they were driving to pick her up at her hotel.

"She drives me crazy, but if anything went wrong, I'd want her there."

"Do you expect something to go wrong?"

"I hope not, but this case has been troublesome from the start."

"True. You know, she could've stayed at my place. Or yours, and you at mine."

"She prefers the hotel, and her client's paying for it."

"Oh, I didn't know."

Denton sank down in his seat and stared out the window. After their midnight jaunt to the cemetery, he'd slept in and then spent a good part of the day working on the website. Joy had called and given him the go-ahead and sent a few temporary graphics.

Several photos of Eugene Kent had arrived in Denton's mailbox too. Gene had brown hair like Luke Duke, but the similarities ended there. In one of the pictures, Gene and Will stood shoulder to shoulder in front of a white-shingled house. Gene's arm lay casually draped over Will's shoulder, and both smiled at the photographer, whose shadow invaded the bottom of the frame.

Bran had spent the day at the County Clerk's office and then meeting his mother. The death record complemented the information from Rosemary Dankworth. Willard Hayes had drowned in his own bathtub on December 25, 1972. The coroner had ruled the death accidental, noting high levels of alcohol and benzodiazepine in Willard's blood.

Prescription Valium had been found in the apartment. Those details fit with the sounds they had heard in the bathroom.

"It could've been suicide," Denton had said when he'd read the report.

Bran had disagreed. "There was no note, and suicide victims are usually clothed. He was naked."

Denton couldn't even imagine how Will must have felt losing his best friend, possibly lover, in such a way, and right before the holidays. He wished he could go back in time and fix it for them. Right, time machine—he needed to start working on it.

"You're quiet. What's wrong?" Bran asked.

"Just thinking."

Denton looked at Bran, really looked. He took inventory of Bran's features—sensuous lips, harsh cheekbones, strong brows, and intense, dark eyes. They all added up to something strange yet intimately familiar, all of them manifestations of the complicated person beneath. A funny twinge in his solar plexus told Denton he more than liked this man.

Bran must've noticed him staring. At the next red light, he turned to Denton. "What's on your mind?"

"Do you have plans for Christmas?" Denton burst out. "I'm afraid to ask about Layla," he added.

"She'll spend it partying in the desert with her pagan friends. I've already asked."

"How about you?"

"I have nothing planned. You?"

"I'll spend it with Mom and my stepdad. I'd love it if you joined me. I can't promise much excitement, though."

Bran being quiet was nothing new, but the blush over his cheeks was, and Denton didn't know how to interpret it. So he waited.

"You really want me to?" Bran asked at long last.

"Yes! With you there, I won't be bored out of my skull, and I'll also get Mom off my back about never bringing anyone home. Please come!" He truly wanted to Bran to join him. He wanted spend Christmas with the people he loved the most.

The impatient wail of a car horn cut their exchange short—the light had turned green.

"All right, I will." Bran said, putting the car in gear. "Thank you." A shy smile played on his lips as he glanced at Denton.

Layla waited for them at the curb. When Denton hopped out of the car, she gave him a lavender-scented hug. He happily returned the embrace, then squeezed himself into the backseat so she could sit up front.

"How was your…umm, meeting? About a merger, right?" he asked as Bran eased back into the traffic.

She turned in her seat. "Enlightening. We found out that the accountant at the other company has been cooking the books."

"How?" Denton had no idea witchcraft could be so useful in business dealings.

"He admitted it during the meeting."

"Just like that?"

Layla winked. "It must've weighed heavily on his conscience. The copal incense burning in my client's office and a few well-placed spells helped him to unburden."

"Ah, copal. I must remember that trick."

They spent the rest of the trip chattering about the pros and cons of various compelling spells. Layla did most of the talking, but Denton supplied her with plenty of questions. Bran barely opened his mouth till they arrived at their destination.

"Here we are," was all he said even then.

***

They could hear the water filling up the tub from the moment they stepped through the door. Of course, the bathroom, along with the rest of the condo, still stood empty and dry as a desert. They set up in the living room. Bran and Denton had agreed to stick with the previous night's ritual, substituting graveyard dust for powdered sugar. The dirt sat in a large Tupperware container among the rest of the summoning supplies.

Bran and Layla took their positions as observers at the sides, while Denton mentally ran through the process. He rolled his shoulders in the way of a fighter getting ready for a match. Taking a deep breath, he began the summoning. The photo of Will and Gene together went in the middle of the drop cloth. Denton encircled it with dirt and went on chanting and drawing symbols much the same as before. This time, though, when he drew the signs of conjuration in the air and demanded the spirits to appear, Will complied immediately. He popped out of thin air, semiopaque and agitated.

"Was that the doorbell?" he started straightaway, like the broken record he was.

He flung himself toward the door but couldn't leave the circle. He stood there in a ghostly state of bafflement.

Denton heard Layla gasp, but he kept his eye on the ghost. "Will, do you remember me?"

Right off, he knew it had been a mistake. Will revved up again. "What are you doing here? Where's Gene? He should be here by now."

Denton closed his eyes to shut out the pitiful expression and anxiety of the ghost. He turned all his focus to contacting Gene. He felt a stirring in the distance, and he reached for it with his mind. He stretched as far as he could, into murky darkness, but Gene remained just outside of his grasp, and the effort drained him. Something else reached back, though, coiled around Denton's thoughts, and gave a tug. Denton didn't feel frightened, but he knew he should. Whatever had gotten hold of him didn't mean well. Before he could find out more, a solid presence materialized behind him.

As Bran's arms encircled and anchored him, Denton felt his strength return. Concentrating hard on the image of the smiling Eugene Kent, he reached again and willed the spirit to appear. Heat and light surged through him, and the thing from the dark let go with a snap. Denton's knees buckled, but Bran held him steady.

Denton opened his eyes and saw Gene inside the dirt circle—far more ethereal than Will but still recognizable. The two ghosts had no problem seeing each other. Bran and Denton took a couple of quiet steps backward.

Will's happy smile made him shimmer. "You're here."

"I said I'd come, didn't I?" Gene had a deep, resonant voice, like church bells.

Furrows gathered on Will's forehead. "I thought…something happened and you'd never come. But I had to keep waiting." His whole figure wavered.

Gene laid a hand on Will's shoulder. "I know, but I'm here now."

Will stilled. "And you'll stay? For good?"

"Yes, my love. You and I, till the end of eternity."

"Oh, Gene, I love you so much." The soft glow around Gene got stronger and spread to Will.

"I know." Gene stepped closer and cradled Will's face with his hands. Their eyes locked, and as they stood very still, their bodies melded into each other. Gene leaned forward. As they kissed, their bodies gradually faded away till they were no more than a wisp of smoke, and then not even that. An inexplicable breeze swept through the room, blowing out all the candles at once.

None of them spoke for a good while, but Layla didn't try to hide her sniffles. Denton furiously avoided looking at Bran. Witnessing the intimacy of the ghostly lovers made him feel raw. Words were awkward, clumsy things, and he was afraid of saying something wrong. He needed a little time to get his balance back. Bran didn't appear any more talkative as they wrapped up their supplies and cleaned up all signs of their visit in silence.

Denton was glad to be out of the condo and into the crisp November air. The stars twinkled in the clear night sky as much as the city's light pollution let them. Cars rushed around, and a few blocks away, an alarm wailed. Life went on.

Layla busied herself at the back of the car, arranging things in the trunk the way she thought they ought to be, so Denton took the opportunity to steal a kiss from Bran. The trunk lid slammed shut, and they flew apart.

"You boys did well," she said coming around the car. "I was right about you two."

"Right about what?" Bran asked.

"You make each other stronger. You should always remember that." She clapped her hands together. "I'm starving. Who's up for dinner? My treat."

Bran grinned. "I could eat."

***

They settled on an Indian restaurant half a block from Layla's hotel. A sense of accomplishment brightened their mood, and the addition of a bottle of wine unwound them even more. Bran, taking his role as the designated driver seriously, didn't drink, but even he loosened up. He and Layla didn't have a cross word the whole evening. When they walked her back to the hotel, she took her place between them, and they strolled down the street arm in arm in arm. Before saying their good-byes, she extracted a promise from both of them to visit her in LA soon.

Denton still floated on high spirits when he and Bran got home. "You're my knight in shiny armor, you know," he said stepping out of the elevator.

"You're drunk."

"I'm tipsy. There's a difference. How did you know I needed your help? I don't think I could've summoned Gene without you."

"You dropped the wand and went rigid. Plus, Mother practically shoved me at you." Bran unlocked his door. "C'mon, I'll make you coffee."

Denton followed him into the apartment and took a deep breath. He'd started to associate the scent of herbs with home and comfort. "I should just move in. I spend most my time over here anyway," Denton said as they hung up their coats and kicked off their shoes.

"Why don't you?" Bran asked matter-of-factly.

Denton didn't expect that reply. Bran had struck him as someone who liked his space and privacy. "You mean it?"

"I do. You could at least bring over more of your stuff. I'll make room."

Bran turned into the kitchen and busied himself with the coffeemaker. Denton watched him from the doorway.

"I don't have much stuff."

"That'll only make it easier."

"You're serious."

"Sure. I'm always serious, remember?" Bran switched the machine on and turned around.

Denton hummed. "Nah, not always. Somewhere deep down, under all the black and grim, you're a barrel of fun waiting to break out. Or was it a barrel of monkeys?"

Bran's lips curled up. "You're a barrel of something, all right."

Denton realized Bran had been smiling more these days—it turned his normally solemn expression almost playful. Denton closed the distance between them and put both arms around Bran. "You're a beautiful man."

It tickled him to see the blush turning Bran's olive complexion to a darker shade. Pressing his advantage, he slid his hands lower, to Bran's buttocks. "I hate these baggy jeans. I wish you wore kilts instead, like I suggested. You're part Welsh, right?"

"One-fourth."

"Enough. The Welsh wear kilts. I looked it up. You should try, at least at home."

"Okay, I will. If you do too." Bran gave the picture of a man feeling rather smart and satisfied with himself.

Denton riposted, "Deal!"

Bran's face fell.

"Ha! You didn't think I would agree, did you? I'm not ashamed of my body, even if it's not much."

Bran's arms effortlessly surrounded Denton's skinny frame. "I find your body one hundred percent sexy."

"Pervert." Denton slipped a hand into Bran's jeans to rub the base of the tail. He'd learned that its underside was especially responsive to stimulation. He needed to get Bran out of those damn jeans. "Bedroom," he commanded.

"I thought I was the captain," Bran complained.

"It's a mutiny. Now move." Denton pinched Bran's bum, then shoved him toward the door.

Bran muttered something about subordination and put up a token resistance. On the way to the bedroom, it turned into a tussle and pulling at each other's clothing. They fell over onto the bed and continued to wrestle. Sort of. They would've been disqualified from any professional event and arrested for gross public indecency. In the end, Denton pinned Bran down, though simply because Bran let him. By then Denton only had his briefs and socks on. Bran's shirt lay open, revealing his naked torso, and his jeans dangled around his ankles.

Denton straddled Bran and held his lover's wrists down, using all his negligible weight. "You're my prisoner and better do as I say, or I'll throw you in the brig. Understood?"

Bran kept the game going. "What will you do with me?"

"First I'll ravage you—standard procedure," Denton said with his best lecherous leer.

Bran blinked a few times before finding his voice. "Is it what you want?"

"It's what I'd like, but not if you don't."

While Denton waited for a reply, he saw a jumble of emotions stir in Bran's eyes.

Bran nodded. "Okay."

Denton pressed a kiss on Bran's lips. "Just go with the flow, babe."

Bran snorted, probably at the impromptu pet name.

Denton licked and nibbled his way down Bran's chest, to the belly button, then down the aptly named treasure trail. Bran's dick strained against the cotton of the jockstrap. Denton took a mental note to look online for kinky versions of this type of underwear, maybe something in leather. He mouthed the thick shaft through the fabric at first. The growing wet spot signaled him to up the stakes. He stripped Bran naked and divested himself of his undies too, while he was at it. He kept his red-and-yellow-striped socks on. They were the same pair he'd worn when he'd first had his way with Bran—his lucky pair since.

Denton gave Bran's dick and balls equal attention, using his tongue stud to full effect. It was his specialty, and he wanted to remind Bran how good that small piece of metal could feel at the right spot. Judging from Bran's labored breathing and hands rubbing Denton's head, he was doing well. He turned his attention to Bran's tail. Bran, who'd grown up hiding his extra appendage, had at first been shocked by Denton's interest and rather shy about it. However, Denton's insistence had worn him down.

Denton licked the length of the tail, from tip to base. He took the opportunity to steal his tongue between Bran's cheeks. The moment he touched Bran's hole, Bran went rigid, and he gripped Denton's hair. Denton, though, didn't back off, and as he continued his ministrations, the tension gradually drained from Bran's muscles. When the tip of

Denton's finger slipped inside, Bran tensed only a little and soon relaxed.

Sitting up, Denton saw Bran stretched out on the sheets, head thrown back and his arm covering his face. Denton knew how difficult this had to be for him—it must have taken all his trust to so completely give up control.

A rush of emotions flooded Denton's chest, making it hard to breathe. He'd make this as good for Bran as he could. Instead of going for the small sachet in the pocket of his jeans, Denton took the whole bottle of lube from the night-table drawer. He opened Bran with the greatest care and gentleness, with his lips around Bran's cock or balls the whole time, for maximum distraction. Too successfully.

Bran pulled at Denton's hair. "I'll come if you don't stop."

Denton quickly stopped. "No. Not yet. I'm not done ravaging."

Bran took his arm from over his eyes. "Well, get on with it already." The hoarseness of his voice belied the bold words.

As the head of Denton's cock slipped through the first ring of resistance, Bran responded with a throaty groan. His chest rose and fell like he was running a marathon, but his breath caught as Denton hit his gland.

Denton pulled back and pushed in again. He'd been on the receiving end of such a bonking before, so he knew how his Prince Albert—a fine curved barbell with round beads at each end—enhanced the sensation. He moved slowly at first, but then he snapped his hips forward and watched Bran's eyes roll back. It made him pretty pleased with himself.

Something unexpected made Denton lose rhythm. He stopped midthrust as a slender but solid thing penetrated his ass. "Oh, you…" He gaped at Bran in disbelief.

It was Bran's turn to look smug. "Go with the flow, *babe*," he said, as he slipped his tail farther inside Denton.

"Mmm…there," Denton moaned as the tip found his sensitive spot.

He made an experimental move with his hips, and it felt heavenly. In no time, they found their rhythm again. Denton knew he should've been concentrating on Bran's pleasure, but the double sensation of fucking Bran and being fucked by Bran's tail short-circuited his brain. Bran's body going taut and clamping around him proved to be the last straw, and Denton came with a loud groan too.

***

"You're full of tricks, aren't you?" Denton asked once he got his breathing and heart rate back to normal.

"Demons are tricksters, I've told you."

Bran fished a pillow out of the tangle of bedding, folded it in half, and tucked it under his head. Denton used Bran's chest for the same purpose.

"You're still wearing your socks," Bran said with amusement.

Denton lifted up a foot and wiggled his toes. "They're my lucky pair."

"Yeah, I remember. You wore them when you first ravaged me."

"You do?" It surprised him that Bran would recall such a small detail.

"I have a pretty good memory, and your socks are hard to forget." Bran traced the tips of his fingers up and down Denton's bicep.

"I have a lot of them," Denton noted, lowering his foot.

"I counted twenty-one pairs."

"Good. You and Joy will have something to talk about when we go over for Thanksgiving dinner."

Bran went stiff. "We do what-when-where?"

"Oh, I thought I'd mentioned it already. Joy invited us to spend turkey day with her." Denton tilted his head to get a better view of Bran's face.

"No, you definitely didn't mention it," Bran grumbled.

"Well, I'm telling you now. She threatened to cook, so we better bring dessert and several bottles of wine. Oh yeah, we should also wear our new utility kilts. I found this awesome online store. We can get them in time if we order now. Might have to do express delivery."

"I'm not going to dinner at your friend's house wearing a skirt," Bran protested.

"Joy won't mind at all. She'll get a kick out of it, if anything."

"No. Way."

Denton sighed. "Fine. We'll go wearing boring old jeans. Happy?"

"Over the moon," Bran said, giving Denton a glare full of suspicion.

It was probably dawning on him that he'd just tacitly agreed to go to the dinner. *Well played.* Denton secretly congratulated himself but kept an expression of innocence on his face. Demons weren't the only tricksters.

Bran shook his head and rolled out of the bed. "I need a shower."

Denton hopped after him. "I'll scrub your tail!"

THE END

About the Author

Under a prickly, cynical surface Lou Harper is an incorrigible romantic. Her love affair with the written word started at a tender age. There was never a time when stories weren't romping around in her head. She is currently embroiled in a ruinous romance with adjectives. In her free time Lou stalks deviant words and feral narratives.

Lou's favorite animal is the hedgehog. She likes nature, books, movies, photography, and good food. She has a temper and mood swings.

Lou has misspent most of her life in parts of Europe and the US, but is now firmly settled in Los Angeles and worships the sun. However, she thinks the ocean smells funny. Lou is a loner, a misfit, and a happy drunk.

Web site: http://louharper.com
Blog: http://louharper.blogspot.com

Other Books by Lou Harper

Spirit Sanguine

© 2012 Lou Harper

Is that a wooden stake in your pocket, or are you just happy to see me?

After five years in eastern Europe using his unique, inborn skills to slay bloodsuckers, Gabe is back in his hometown Chicago and feeling adrift. Until he's kidnapped by a young, sexy vampire who seems more interested in getting into his pants than biting into his neck.

Harvey Feng is one-half Chinese, one-hundred-percent vampire. He warns Gabe to stay out of the Windy City, but somehow he isn't surprised when the young slayer winds up on his doorstep. And why shouldn't Gabe be curious? A vegetarian vampire isn't something one sees every day.

Against their better judgment, slayer and vampire succumb to temptation. But their affair attracts unexpected attention.

When Chicago's Vampire Boss makes Gabe an offer he can't refuse, the unlikely lovers are thrust into peril and mystery in the dark heart of the Windy City. Together they hunt for kidnappers, a killer preying on young humans, and vicious vampire junkies.

However, dealing with murderous humans and vampires alike is easy compared to figuring out if there's more to their   relationship   than   hot,   kinky   sex.

Warning: Fangalicious man-on-man action, a troublesome twink, cross-dressing vampiress, and role-playing involving a fedora.

Enjoy this excerpt from Spirit Sanguine:

It was Gabe's thirteenth straight perfect summer night in Chicago since he'd arrived back from Budapest. He left his cheap hotel in Rogers Park and headed downtown. The air was as smooth as fine red wine, and the moon hung in the sky like a fat lump of Camembert. It felt strange being back home after all those years. The city was essentially the same as he'd left it, but he'd changed and no longer fit in. The odd sensation of being a stranger in his hometown made him restless.

As it was Friday night, the streets of River North were teeming with tourists and locals. Gabe popped in and out of bars, not staying long anywhere. He had a few beers, but it would've taken something stronger than alcohol to fill the void inside him. He stalked the streets at night because he didn't know what else to do. Coming home had been a logical and necessary step, but he had no idea what came next. To make things worse, he hadn't gotten laid for far too long. Not that there was a shortage of willing bodies. Gabe knew he didn't stand out in a crowd, but he had no problem attracting guys, especially ones who liked a bit of rough trade. Dark-haired and sturdy, he had the physique and air of a man who could give that to them. So there were plenty of interested men, just none of them "lit his fire". Truth be told, he was in the granddaddy of all funks.

Gabe would never in a million years have expected to find someone to answer all his yearnings at once. The young man who bumped into him in the crowded bar murmured hasty apologies and walked away. As collisions went, it seemed as innocuous as the first contact between the Titanic and the errant iceberg, yet at the moment of contact, Gabe's heart hurled itself at his rib cage, sensing the impending disaster. As they parted, he stared after the other figure: short, slender, dark-haired and undead. A killer combo. It was unfair; the most fuckable ass he'd come across in who knew how long, and it belonged to a vampire.

Gabe had a sixth sense for these things, quite literally. In the proximity of a vampire, his skin prickled and the short hairs on the back of his neck stood at attention. At the same time, an invisible compass in his brain zeroed in on the creature. Oddly, in this instance the sensation was as faint as the brush of a spider web, yet still unmistakable. To clinch it, Mr. Killer Buns was several degrees too cool to the touch.

Finding and slaying vampires was Gabe's special skill, one might even say calling, although he'd been having second thoughts about that as of late. The current situation was most disturbing; thoughts of sex and vampires had never before occupied his brain at the same time. The undead he and his uncle had been hunting across Europe for the past several years hadn't inspired such notions. They'd been a revolting bunch that without fail had tried to rip out his throat. Not one of them had worn tight jeans showing off shapely buttocks.

"The only good vampire is a dead vampire," Uncle Miklos used to say. So Gabe sent the carnal thoughts packing and concentrated on the task ahead. It had to be done. Pity.

When his mark left the bar, Gabe followed at a prudent distance all the way to the El station. Since he saw no trains coming, Gabe waited a minute before walking up to the platform. He spotted his target at the far end, so he stayed back. It wasn't yet time to make his move. He was going to follow the vamp back to its nest where there might be more of its kind. Minutes ticked by. Gabe took a few casual glances at the creature. It seemed oblivious, chatting on a cell phone. Gabe wondered who was on the other end of the line. The bloodsuckers he'd had experience with were neither particularly social nor technologically savvy.

The train finally arrived, and they got on. A good twenty minutes later when the vampire got off, Gabe followed, waiting till the last minute to jump off. The vamp had already walked down the stairs and out of sight, but Gabe could still feel its presence. He tracked it on deserted, dimly lit streets. He tugged down the zipper of his leather jacket and slipped his hand inside. Three wooden stakes sat on each side in their custom-designed holders. Old habits died hard.

Gabe caught a movement in the shadows from the corner of his eye, but it didn't alarm him much—the only undead in the area was half a block ahead. The sudden sharp sting in his posterior took him completely by surprise. After a moment of confusion, he yanked the dart out and stared at it. Why would somebody shoot him with a dart? As his knees turned to jelly and the world faded away, he understood he'd probably made the last mistake of his life.

Gabe came to in an empty, windowless room, lit by a bare lightbulb hanging from the ceiling. The mold-stained walls amplified the low-budget-horror-flick ambiance. The one thing out of synch was the bloodsucker crouched in front of him—it looked at him with concern morphing into relief as Gabe clawed his way back to consciousness. Now that he got a closer look at it, the vampire proved to be even more intriguing; its features were an appealing fusion of Asian and Caucasian. The eyes staring at Gabe were brown around the iris, blending into green. It was, without question, the most attractive vampire Gabe had ever seen. But that wasn't saying much.

Gabe knelt on the cold concrete floor, propped against the wall in an uncomfortable position, but when he tried to move, he realized he was expertly bound—ankles together, hands behind his back, and all tied together, so he couldn't even stand up.

"You're a slayer, right?" the vampire asked, more curious than accusatory.

Gabe had no intention of giving in that easy. "I don't know what you're talking about. I was walking home when you kidnapped me. It's a federal crime, you know."

"And you simply happened to have six very sharp wooden sticks on you. Or were you just happy to see me?"

For the first time ever, Gabe witnessed a vampire smirk. It perturbed him more than a vicious scowl would've.

Looking down, he also became aware of not wearing his jacket anymore. Well, the gig was up. Still, he wasn't going to make this any easier for the bastard; he clamped his jaws together and said nothing.

The vampire sighed. "Don't be a grumpy pants. Let's say we agree you're a slayer."

"And you're a soulless bloodsucker." Gabe produced a scowl appropriate for the circumstances, but he started to get a strange feeling that they weren't working from the same script.

The vampire wasn't bothered. "Sticks and stones. Tell me, where did you come from? You're new here, right? We haven't had a slayer around here in ages. What brought you here now?" It looked at Gabe as if he were the Easter Bunny.

Gabe figured it made no difference, but he might as well make up some pretty lies. "Fine, you got me. My buddies and I are new in town. I was supposed to meet them. They're probably looking for me."

The vampire cocked its head sideways and studied him for a second. "Nah. You're lying."

Gabe shrugged as much as the ropes allowed. "Maybe. Or maybe not."

The vampire chewed on its fingernails while studying Gabe silently some more. "You're a pain in the ass," it said.

Gabe stared back in his best Bruce Willis impression, but inside he felt flummoxed. He'd been insulted by vampires before but never so benignly. Threats of getting ripped from limb to limb were more along the line of what he'd been expecting. This was a strange fucking night.

The vampire leaned forward and put a hand over Gabe's heart. Its eyelids drifted closed, and its curvy lips parted slightly, as if in a trance, creating a positively sensuous picture. It almost made Gabe regret what he was about to do. Almost. Putting all his strength and weight into it, he launch himself forward and head-butted the vampire. Having been knocked back on its pretty ass, it looked startled for a nanosecond, but then in a flash it was in Gabe's face, fangs bared, eyes burning with amber fury. It put a hand around Gabe's throat and squeezed while sliding its other hand under Gabe's shirt, fingers digging into naked skin.

"Give me a good reason why I shouldn't disembowel you?" the vampire hissed.

Dead in L.A.

© 2012 Lou Harper

Trouble comes in deceptive packages

Still recovering from an accident that left him emotionally and physically battered, Jon's goal is to lead a simple life, free of complications and attachments. His new roommate—a happy-go-lucky bookworm—seems to fit into his plans fine at first. He doesn't find out till later that Leander's also a psychic, specializing in finding lost pets. Jon's a skeptic when it comes to the supernatural, so he's convinced Leander's a nut job.

Jon's beliefs are challenged when Leander has to track down a missing teenager and he ropes Jon into assisting him. Soon the two of them are knee-deep in a decades-old murder case. The hills and valleys of the City of Angels hold many buried secrets, and Leander has a knack for finding them.

Jon's hopes for a trouble-free life go out the window as he's drawn deeper into Leander's psychic sleuthing. Digging into the past poses many dangers, but the biggest risk Jon faces is putting his bruised heart on the line.

Warning: Men loving men, skeletons, and an unlucky Chihuahua.

Last Stop
© 2012 Lou Harper

Sam Mayne's life is as dull as the dishwater in his small-town Montana diner, and that's just how he wants it. Quiet, uneventful, safe from his shadowy past. The breezy young drifter who answers his help-wanted ad makes him uneasy in ways he dare not examine too closely. Except he can't help but be pulled in by Jay Colby's spunky attitude, endless stories, and undeniable sex appeal.

Fresh off yet another romantic disaster, Jay doesn't understand his attraction to the taciturn line cook, but there's no fighting the chemistry that lands them in bed together. Where Sam's subtly dominant streak takes command, and Jay delights in discovering the pleasures of his submissive side.

Safe in the assumption their relationship is temporary, neither lover holds back when the heat is on. Until Sam's deadly past catches up with them with a vengeance, forcing him to drop the life he's built, pick up his lover, and run. As danger cuts closer to the bone, Sam and Jay are forced to face the truth. About themselves, about the depth of their love—and the newly forged bonds that are about to be tested to the limit.

Warning: Contains enough sparks to ignite a sexual fire, ably fanned by the judicious use of some interesting props, as well as some butt-warming spanking. Sizzzzzle.

Made in the USA
San Bernardino, CA
13 August 2013